S0-AXN-734

LOW BRIDGE

A Saga of Ohio's Miami-Erie Canal

By
Nioma Stephan

Illustrated By
Kathryn Rees

PublishAmerica
Baltimore

© 2005 by Nioma Stephan.
All rights reserved. No part of this book may be reproduced, stored in a retrieval system or transmitted in any form or by any means without the prior written permission of the publishers, except by a reviewer who may quote brief passages in a review to be printed in a newspaper, magazine or journal.

First printing

This is a work of fiction. The time, place, and canal information are all historical.

ISBN: 1-4137-9957-4
PUBLISHED BY PUBLISHAMERICA, LLLP
www.publishamerica.com
Baltimore

Printed in the United States of America

This book could not have been completed without the help of many.

My thanks goes to:
Ray Zunk, The Authors Alliance, Kathryn Rees, Lucille Hetzel, Dorothy Hertenstein, Donald and Angela Hoehn, James Oda, Betty McKowen, Andy Hite, my family and friends who continually encouraged me.

Dedication
To:
My mother's parents
Henry and Freda Utrup.
My parents
Kenneth and Edna Kortokrax.
My Deitering children,
and their families.
As well as
my husband,
Robert Stephan

Elevation Chart

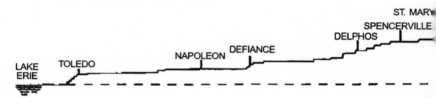

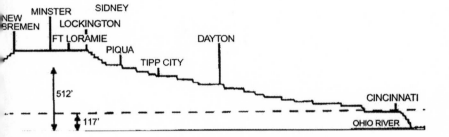

This chart was created by the Department of Natural Resources-
Division of Water, Columbus, Ohio

Author's Note

Sometimes on this earth, like the delicate rose, life starts with the thought of the beauty to come. The root is planted, takes hold in the earth and is nurtured.

There are thorns and blights but it grows until it flourishes; becomes a thing of beauty.

It blooms with all its heart in deep rich color dulling its surroundings in comparison. For a short time it is the only thing noticeable.

Then like the delicate rose, another beauty raises its head and the rose petals start to wilt. Its color loses its luster and eventually its life blood returns to the earth. Mother Nature blows a storm in the wind, and it's as though the rose was never there. The American Canal System was like that.

Prologue

1803

The new state of Ohio was isolated from every avenue that could possibly give it any future growth. Still it had many potential investors convinced that the interior of Ohio could be profitable.

Wild animals, Indians, along with occasional frontiersman and small groups of settlers along the Ohio River populated the region.

Those few settlers were getting amazing yields of wheat and corn. They had pigs and chickens in abundance, cut their own lumber, and were successful at trapping furs.

The market in New York was begging for such goods. A passageway through that wilderness was definitely needed.

1825

In 1825 the Governor of New York, DeWitt Clinton, broke ground for a canal system in Ohio. It was an extremely complicated plan consisting of two main canals running mostly north to south, and going the length of the state, from Lake Erie to the Ohio River. The Miami-Erie Canal was one of those.

By the year 1845 the Miami & Erie Canal which started at the Ohio River, continued northward through Middletown, Dayton, Piqua, Lockington, Spencerville, Delphos, Ottoville, Defiance, Maumee and other villages, past Toledo and into Lake Erie where it ended.

The following story is about the building of that canal and about the canal people of that era: why they lived as they did, their joys, heartbreaks, and their daydreams. It is about their deep faith in God, and their desire to be free from the political and economical oppression of their homeland in Europe

Contents

PART FOUR

PART ONE

CHAPTER 1
SCHINBONE, OHIO October 1825
A Lost Child

"Something's wrong." Gertrude pushed the quilted blanket back from her wool-covered feet. She shook her husband, Joseph. "Wake up. Wake up!"

Almost immediately he awoke from a sound sleep, jumped from the wooden rope bed, and reached for the wax candle to put in his wife's hand. While she lit the candle using the bright red coals still smoldering in the fireplace, he quickly took his gun down from the cabin wall, loaded it, and cautiously opened the heavy plank door a crack.

"Who's there?" Joseph called while his dogs continued to bark viciously. He held his gun steady. "Who's there?" he repeated. Joseph heard a wailing cry. Straining to hear better he opened the door a bit more with his foot, then spoke harshly to his dogs. "Quiet!"

From the cloudless sky, small patches of moonlight fell through the thick forest.

Joseph strained to see until his eyes became accustomed to the shadows of the night. Then he saw a child sitting on the hard-packed dirt. Not believing, he squeezed his eyes shut and then opened them again.

"It is a child!" he said, his voice soft, though full of astonishment. He opened the door a bit further so that his wife could see.

Searching through the now quiet night, Gertrude looked past the sitting figure and called. "Who's there?"

The small head turned to look up at her. Her fear and hatred of the close, dark wilderness, since they'd arrived five years earlier from Germany, prevented her from moving toward the child. She set the candle holder on the wide plank floor and knelt down holding out her large hands. "Come," she pleaded. "We have some milk."

The child, unsure and trembling, got up slowly on its feet and moved toward the dimly lit doorway, pausing several feet from Gertrude's open arms. Slowly, the tired child trudged forward on its short, heavily clad legs.

CHAPTER 2
The Child Finds a Home

Joseph, in his long nightshirt, with his back against the bolted door, looked at his wife in her heavy nightgown. She held the child's mitten-covered hand.

Once more he squeezed shut his blue eyes and opened them again. The child was still there.

How did this child come to us by itself, in this forest and in the middle of the night? he asked himself.

Meager warmth still radiated from the dying coals as Joseph slowly stirred the embers. He added two small logs, and the flames leapt to life.

"What do we do?" he asked his wife, who still held the mitten-covered hand.

The child, with a tear-stained face, had not made a sound, not even a whimper.

It must be terribly afraid, Joseph thought, as he stood tall to straighten his aching back.

In front of the fireplace Gertrude sat down slowly on the hardwood rocker. Gently she began to take the mittens off of the small hands. "Can you fetch us a cup of milk?" she asked Joseph.

"Bread too?" he asked.

She nodded and began to hum a quiet little tune while she unbuttoned the dark woolen coat that covered the small breast. Laying it aside she gently lifted the child up onto her spacious lap, put her arms around its middle and laid her hands lightly on those of the child. She rocked silently.

Eventually she took the knitted stocking cap, smelling of autumn leaves, from the blond head.

Joseph looked at them when he brought the tin cup filled with milk. He'd placed a slice of fresh bread Gertrude had made that morning on a wooden plate. Butter covered the inner part of the crusted piece.

She looks happy holding the child, he thought. He held the cup in front of them. Tiny hands reached to take it. Gertrude's and Joseph's eyes met; the child trusted them.

After one long drink the cup was empty. A smile covered the child's face as the bread passed his lips

"More milk?" Joseph asked.

The child nodded its head. Happily Joseph went for more milk. Later, after Gertrude had washed the child with a warm, wet cloth, she slipped one of Joseph's shirts over the boy child.

"Show him where to pee," she said to her husband.

The red-bearded man and the boy went together to the far corner of the room to the pot hidden behind the tall chest. Shortly the three slept soundly, the boy nestled between the two.

CHAPTER 3
Carnage

In the early morning in the forest, less than a mile from the cabin, the sight before Joseph took his breath away. A dead, fully-grown gray wolf lay at the edge of the narrow footpath. It had been shot. Cautiously, he touched it with the tip of his gun.

Twenty feet further, a gun lay against a tree. A battered lantern lay on its side. There were wolf tracks and a disheveled forest floor. His stomach rolled.

A pack of wolves divided and came at them from the side and from the back, he thought. He looked about and wondered aloud. "How did the boy escape?"

Seeing the remains of two human forms he retched. Moments later, still feeling sick in his body, he gathered the few belongings he'd found and put them in his knapsack. He picked up their gun and lantern.

Slivers of daylight began to filter through the trees as he made his way back to the cabin. *The boy must have escaped the attack, but how did he do it?*

At home Joseph went to the shed where he laid down the gun and lantern he'd found. He picked up his pick and shovel and put them on his shoulder. Carrying his own gun in his free hand, he went back into the forest.

An hour later he was home again, pale and sweaty. He washed at the well. With heavy footsteps, his knapsack still on his back, he returned to their one-room cabin. Joseph knew it would take another trip out to the woods to the grizzly scene for the re-gathering of the body parts that he had so quickly buried. It was indecent and anti-Christian to bury adults in unnamed graves in the forest. As soon as possible, he vowed they would be buried in a church yard.

CHAPTER 4
Maternal Love

Having the child made Trudy happy. This morning she smiled and hummed delightful tunes that Joseph could not remember hearing in months. She lovingly brushed the boy's blond hair that fell over his eyes, covered his ears, and curled at the nape of his neck.

He must be about four years old, Joseph thought as he quietly placed his gun back into the gun rack and set the gun powder and shot on the shelf below. Loosening the straps of the knapsack, he set it on the table. As he did so the cover flipped back and the chain of a gold pocket watch slipped out.

Trudy laid the hair brush down, and taking the boy's hand led him over to Joseph. The boy still had not spoken.

To Joseph, Trudy mouthed the words, "Ask him his name."

It seemed like a natural question to ask, but Joseph hesitated. He pulled a chair out from the table. At ease, he sat down. "My name is Joseph, and this is Trudy," he said softly to the boy. "What is your name?"

The boy, seeking the protection of Trudy, edged closer to the soft long folds of her dress. He looked at Joseph with uncertainty, and then his eyes turned upwards at Trudy for reassurance. She smiled and nodded her head. Again, he looked at Joseph.

"Adam," the boy said.

So pleased was Trudy that she knelt to give him a hug. "Are you three years old, Adam?"

He shook his head.

"Four?" Joseph asked.

Adam thought, then smiled in agreement. As quickly as he'd accepted them he became wary. Joseph and Trudy saw the look in his eyes. Immediately Joseph changed tactics.

"I'm hungry," he said. "Are you hungry, Adam?"

"Yes," the small boy said nodding his head.

Trudy went to the fireplace to add a log to the already warm hearth and to put the water kettle on its hook at the edge of the blaze. Joseph picked up the knapsack to clear the table, and took it over to the tall chest near the bed. He opened the top drawer and gently placed the sack's contents into it. An hour later Joseph left the cozy cabin, fully dressed for the cold. His powder horn was strung around his waist and his gun was in hand. The empty knapsack was on his back as he headed toward the shed.

As he walked, he glanced around this acreage they called Freedom with new awareness. *What had the place looked and sounded like through the eyes and ears of Adam, alone, frightened and exhausted, as he must have been in the middle of the night?*

Would Adam have seen the pump sticking out of the wood platform on the top of the hand-dug well? Would the moonlight in the darkness, have cast odd shaped, scary shadows? Was he used to the sounds of birds twittering, of owls hooting, and flocks of larger birds flapping their wings? Would he have recognized the sounds of squirrels scampering up trees, of groundhogs running? Would he know the sound of the wind blowing ever so lightly, bringing down leaves? Would Bessie have mooed, or Dick neighed as the child walked by, or were the dogs barking by then?

Joseph carried several buckets of fresh cold water to the water trough and threw hand-shelled corn to the five hens as they clucked about his boots inside the roughly made barn structure. Sidestepping them he lifted the clean milk pail from the post and then relieved

Bessie of her morning milk. Later he led the two animals into the corral.

He carried the half-full milk pail to the cabin. Again, he thought of Adam. *We are both so taken by him.* Inside he set the milk pail beside the water bucket on the bench behind the door, and said goodbye to Trudy and Adam. On his way out, he picked up the gun he'd brought back in with him.

For an hour he trudged through the woods, checking his traps. His catch amounted to three rabbits for stew. In his mind, he covered the hours since Adam's arrival. Eventually he found himself near Frank and Marta, his closest neighbor. Their dogs began to bark as he approached.

"Hush, dogs," Joseph said.

The dogs recognized his voice, and as he got closer, his smell. They began wagging their tails. Joseph petted their smooth heads. The door opened before he reached it.

Frank Schmidt stood in the doorway, a wide smile covering his face. "Good to see you, Joseph," he said. "Are you out checking your traps or hunting?"

"Doing a little of both. I think I need to talk with you."

"Come in then."

"I'd rather not."

"Let me put my coat on." He disappeared behind the door. Marta, his wife, waved and smiled when she saw him. Their five-year old daughter Annie came to the open door. "Morning, Mr. Gephart," she said, her eyes bright, her blonde hair in braids.

"Good morning Annie."

"Close the door, Annie," Frank said as he stepped in front of her to the outside.

The two men walked in silence to the fence that corralled Frank's farm animals. Side by side, leaning against the rail fence, Frank lit his pipe. "What is it that is bothering you?" he asked.

Joseph looked at him but said nothing, trying to put his thoughts in order. "I don't know where to start."

"At the beginning," said Frank, who was five years older than Joseph.

"In the middle of our sleep last night the dogs started barking." Joseph told him about the arrival of Adam.

Stunned by the tale, Frank forgot to draw on his pipe. He lit it again as Joseph finished. "I poured the contents into the top drawer. I didn't tell Trudy yet."

"Why not?"

"She doesn't know what I found. It has become a problem. The boy is all she sees and thinks about...We have wanted a child for three years and still we have had none. Then out of the forest he comes. It is like Adam is meant for us."

Frank nodded his head.

"The child is not ours," Joseph said, his anxiety showing on his face. "We must take Adam to his family."

"Do you know who that is? Did the boy say?"

"We did not ask. He said only that his name is Adam."

"Were there any papers with the things you picked up in the forest?"

"Not a one," Joseph said, frustrated. "There might have been before the attack, but I didn't find any."

"The things you found, was there a name on any of it?"

"I don't think so, but I wasn't looking for a name."

The air felt damp; the clouds were churning gray, and in the space of the forest clearing, leaves were blowing. Joseph shivered. "It's turning colder." He brushed at his reddened cheeks then turned his conversation back to Adam. "I don't know what to do."

"When you get back and can look through the things, see if there is a name. Without a name you can do nothing, but wait for someone to ask about the boy." He puffed on his pipe. "You might contact the Township Marshall, or you might just act like he belongs to you."

"I must think about this," Joseph said. "For sure the remains must be reburied soon."

Having talked with Frank and at least having a starting point at what to do. Joseph looked and felt much better. "I'll look for a name. Thank you for being a friend, Frank."

"You're welcome," Frank said. With his hand he knocked the bowl of his pipe on the fence. Red tobacco coals fell to the ground. "If the weather doesn't worsen, Marta and I, with Annie and little Ben, will walk over to see you tomorrow to meet your Adam. Maybe Annie can make a friend with him."

"Yes, that would be good. Thank you again." Joseph offered his hand to his neighbor and then headed home.

CHAPTER 5
The Visit

"Why is it wrong to invite Frank and his family to meet Adam?" Joseph asked his wife, who sat protectively holding Adam on her lap. "You and Marta can talk while the children play." He did not miss the guarded look she gave him; still he persisted. "You like them."

"They will not approve!" Trudy said.

"Of Adam? Sure they will."

"We will have to give him back," she said.

"To whom do we give him back?" Joseph asked. "He is ours. Gott has given us this child." He looked at the boy snuggling securely in the warmth of Trudy's embrace. "We will keep him until Gott decides different."

Trudy, not one to doubt the wisdom of God, was taken back by what Joseph had said. "Why would Gott decide different?"

Joseph threw up his arms in frustration. "Woman! We will make Frank and his family welcome. They are our friends and neighbors."

Trudy lowered her head, aware that what Joseph decided was how it would be. "Yah," she said, drained with the fear she felt.

Later while she swept around the hearth, Joseph searched in the large trunk that they had brought with them from Germany, and kept at the foot of their bed.

Adam stood at the end of it, his eyes wide. Joseph moved papers and blankets inside of the trunk. He took small wooden boxes from the trunk and picked up a cloth bag heavy with buttons.

"I want to make a toy. Where is your ball of string, Trudy?" he asked as he took a large black coat button from the bag. "We need string long enough to go round his hands when they are spread wide apart."

Trudy, reaching for the large ball of yarn she had spun said, "That button was from my Mother's dress cape. There is another big one." She took the button from him. "I want to keep this."

Again Joseph looked into the bag. "How about this one?" he asked holding up a large buff-colored bone button. In the middle of it were two small holes slightly off-center.

Trudy nodded, "Yes." She took the open bag from him and gently placed the cape button back inside.

Joseph gave the bone button to Adam who followed him to the table where he measured a length of string and cut it. "That should do." He held the piece of string in his hand. "Do you know why we cut this?" he asked Adam.

The boy shook his head.

"May I have the button?" he asked.

Adam pushed the button towards Joseph.

Moments later Joseph squinted as he playfully exaggerated the task at hand. First he put one end of the string in his mouth, then with his fingers, rolled the end to a point and poked at one of the button holes. "Ach!" He said as the point flattened, and hit the button, but missed the hole. He tried again and again, still not getting it through the buttonhole. Desperately he looked at Adam. "Could you do it?"

Adam nodded his head.

"Goot." Joseph said looking relieved. He shoved the button and string toward the boy who quickly took it.

With sudden shyness he looked up at the two adults. They smiled and nodded at him. Seeing their approval he wet the string in his mouth. Carefully with his little fingers he rolled the end until it was a smooth, sharp point. Again he sought the approval of Joseph and Trudy. Receiving it, he held the button steady and aimed the string toward the hole. The end fell down before it reached the button. With a determined look on his face he tried again.

A wide smile covered the small face when it went through. Trudy and Joseph, both delighted, clapped their hands.

"Can yah put the other end through the hole?" Joseph asked.

Without hesitation Adam did just that.

"Wonderful." Joseph said and reached for the string and button. With much show he put the two ends of string, now on the same side of the button, together and tied them into a knot. He pushed the button to the middle of the string, leaving a loop on each end. Adam watched. Slowly, again for emphasis, Joseph put two fingers through the loop on one end and then did the same with two fingers of his left hand on the other loop. He moved his hands apart and pulled the string taunt. The button bobbed. He gave the string some slack and the button hung limp.

He held tightly to the string in each hand. Flicking his wrist he flipped the button over and over, twisting the string until it was tight on his fingers. He gave the twisted string and button more slack, then again pulled outward with each hand.

The button twirled round and round until the twisted string wound the other way, all the while making the sound of a buzzing bee. Adam's eyes never left the button. After a few minutes of twirling the button, Joseph said he was tired of playing with it.

"Would you like to play, Trudy?" he asked. She nodded and snatched the button from her husband. While she twirled the button the boy looked wistfully on. Finally Trudy said, "I'm tired too," and laid the button on the table.

"Me do?" Adam asked. They nodded. Soon he laughed, completely absorbed in button twirling.

When the dogs began barking they remembered the visitors they expected. Adam, still absorbed, did not hear them.

A few minutes passed before they heard the light knock on the door. Trudy opened it. Annie's small fist was about to pound on the door once more. Trudy smiled at the blonde-haired child and her family, inviting them in from out of the cold wind. Leaves rustled and circled about the clearing behind them. The air felt damp and heavy under the gray sky.

"Feels like snow," Marta commented as she unbuttoned her dark wool cape and handed the heavy covering to Trudy. Frank lifted little Ben from his broad shoulders and stood the two-year old boy on the hard dirt floor.

"You're getting so big, little Ben. Soon you will be walking through the woods instead of riding on my shoulders." He put his finger under the child's chin and grinned at him. The boy smiled back at his father, all the while struggling to pull off his mittens.

Annie went to help him. "Let sister help," she said and unbuttoned his coat, the same one she'd worn as a toddler. Recently her mother had thought about changing the buttons to the opposite side but hadn't yet found the time.

Frank brought along his gun, which he carried for protection. He placed it on the rack above Joseph's gun, his powder on the shelf beside Joseph's. At ease, he hung his coat on a chair. Then from his coat pocket he pulled a small wooden horse he had whittled for Ben.

"Mine," Ben said, and eagerly reached for it.

"What is the name of your horse?" Frank asked holding the horse from Ben at an unreachable distance.

"Mine," little Ben said possessively. "Jack mine!"

"Goot, you know his name," Frank said and handed the boy his toy.

All the while Adam sat on a stool by the fireplace playing with the string and button, paying almost no attention to the visitors.

"Come warm yourself on the rocker," Trudy invited Marta. Hesitantly she introduced Adam.

"Frank has told me of your visitor." Marta said to Trudy. Then she asked Adam, "How old are you?"

Adam looked up at her. He said. "Four."

"My name is Marta Schmidt. What is yours?"

"Adam."

"Do you have a last name?"

Adam, a blank look in his eyes shrugged his shoulders.

31

"My name," she started in again, "is Marta Schmidt." In the midst of woman's conversation Annie came over to stand beside her mother who was now seated in the rocker. "This is my little girl. Her name is Annie Schmidt." Marta turned to her daughter. "This young man is Adam," she said.

"Like Adam in the Bible story?" Annie asked.

"He has the same name, dear."

Adam looked at Annie for a moment then went back to his button. Little Ben walked slowly up to Adam and stood beside him. When Adam did not notice him he put his hand out to touch the twirling button. It caught his small fingers and immediately fell from Adam's grasp to the floor.

Ben started to cry. Adam was surprised from his sudden touch and upset, thinking he had hurt the small boy. "Sorry," he said and reached out toward him.

Ben, with tears sliding down his cheeks, his mouth open to cry, reached for the button and string.

"Want me show you?" Adam asked. Ben immediately stopped crying and nodded his head. Ben, blond like his sister and his parents, watched intently as Adam showed him how.

"You want to do it?" Adam asked.

"Yeth," the boy answered.

Adam got up from the stool and helped the boy sit down. Slowly he took the small horse from Ben and laid it on the floor. Then he put the string around the boy's hands and helped him first to twirl the button until the string was completely twisted, then helped him make it buzz like a bee.

Later the children wanted to go with the men to the barn. Trudy helped Adam with his coat. "Hold his hand," she said to Joseph. "He's not been outside since he came."

Inside the shed the men held the children up so that they could touch the cow, Bessie, and Dick, the work horse. When put down they laughed and ran wildly around on the packed dirt floor of the shed.

Seeing the chickens fly from them in fright they imitated them, unbuttoning their coats enough so they could raise and lower their arms. They looked and acted like the chickens flapping their wings. Both men laughed hard at the sight.

Adam came too close to a rough piece of lumber, and ripped a tear in the lining of his coat. The playfulness ended. Sudden fear showed in his eyes and tears welled.

"It's all right." Joseph said trying to console the boy. But not until they returned to the house to show it to Trudy was he at ease.

"Awk," she said, "'tis a small tear. I'll fix it later."

She looked close at the lining as she took his coat from him. A puzzled looked showed on her face. She folded the coat, put it up, and visited with their friends.

CHAPTER 6
Designed Stitches

Trudy had seemed preoccupied as she visited with the neighbors. Normally reluctant to see them go, today she acted almost glad to see them leave.

"What is wrong with you?" Joseph asked abruptly, even before they finished waving their good-byes and closed their door.

She looked perplexed. "We need to talk after Adam is in bed," she said curtly.

He stood open-mouthed. Never had she talked to him in this manner. As soon as Adam's eyelids closed and Trudy felt he was asleep she motioned to Joseph to come sit close beside her in front of the fireplace. Still feeling out of sorts he did so reluctantly, watching as she picked up her sewing basket, and then Adam's coat on her way to the rocking chair.

She set the sewing basket on the floor beside the chair and turned the coat out on her lap; the wool side down, the lining up.

"What's the matter with you?" Joseph asked, demanding an explanation.

"I noticed something when I looked at the rip in Adam's coat today," she said and motioned for Joseph to look. He got up and stood by her side looking down at the torn hole as she pulled the lining away from the wool. He looked inside the lining.

What is it?" he questioned.

"Paper or something sewed into the lining. Look at these stitches." She pointed to the odd design of stitching made on the lining. "I had to look closely to see it."

She picked up her scissors, her thimble, and her heavy needle. Starting at the bottom of the lining, which was sewn to the coat, she loosened a stitch, then cut it.

Continuing on, she opened the hemline. Finally she lifted the lining and folded it back. Three flat sheets of paper, and a folded, sealed sheet were secured to the lining and sewn within the strange design of stitches.

Joseph stood open-mouthed. "I never would have…"

"Neither would I," she said and cautiously started to loosen the stitching of the design.

CHAPTER 7
Loss and Papers

The papers were turned inward, facing the lining, so as Trudy loosened the stitching the writing still could not be seen.

In the quiet of the night, as she worked, the dogs began barking, startling them. A banging was heard on the door. "Mrs. Gephart, Mrs. Gephart." A voice called. The banging became pounding.

Joseph opened the door as Trudy bundled the coat, putting it under her sewing basket.

"Tess is hav'n her baby," the man said. "You got to come!"

"Adam…" Trudy said, torn with indecision. She stood still momentarily.

"Mrs. Gephart," the man pleaded. "Tess needs you now."

Quickly she rushed to Adam's side, leaned over the sleeping boy and kissed his forehead softly.

She moved to the storage cabinet and picked up her midwife's bag. Sitting down she slipped on her heavy boots. Wrapping a wide, black wool scarf around her fair hair, she took down her heavy coat from the hook beside the front door and buttoned it tightly. Pulling on her gloves, she said, "Let's go."

Joseph followed them out. Tess's husband sat on his horse, waiting.

Joseph put his arms around Trudy and kissed her tenderly on the cheek then helped her up behind the man. "Take care."

"I will," she said. "Adam?" she questioned.

"I will take care of him," Joseph said, assuring her.

She sat behind the man, her feet behind his stirrups, holding on to the neighbor's waist. Within moments only the soft pounding of the horse's hooves and an occasional crack of a branch was all that could be heard.

Joseph returned to the inside of the warm, one-room cabin. It seemed empty until he looked at their bed and saw Adam.

At the fireplace he put a knotted oak log near the back of the fire. *It will burn slow and long,* he thought. Then he picked up the coat and sewing basket. Carefully he turned the lining back, as Trudy had done, so the papers were in full view. Idly, he plucked at the loosened threads, then picked up Trudy's scissors and clipped each stitch until the papers were loose.

He was curious, and automatically turned the papers over. *They look important. I better wait for Trudy,* he thought and laid the pages face down on the dirt floor.

Taking Trudy's needle, he threaded it and sewed the hem of the lining to the back of the coat.

Stiff from the hour of sitting, he slowly picked up the papers from the floor, carried the coat to the wooden peg at the door and hung it there. Going to the chest by the bed he opened the top drawer and carefully let the papers, print side down, slip in on top of the gold watch and other items he'd put there only the morning before.

Taking his nightshirt out from the hook near the head of the bed, he put it on. Minutes later he crawled across their four-year old visitor and lay against the wall beside him.

In the morning when Joseph awoke he turned to look at the sleeping boy. *Already he has changed our lives.*

As though he knew he was being thought about, Adam opened his eyes. "Hi," his little voice greeted Joseph while the rest of his body stretched, like that of a lazy cat.

"Hi, yourself," Joseph said and crawled across the stretching body, affectionately mussing the boy's hair as he did so. As Joseph, looking at his reflection in the small hanging mirror, combed his hair and then his beard, he realized that if he looked in the mirror at the right angle he could see Adam. If Adam did the same he could see Joseph.

"Want to use it?" Joseph asked.

Adam nodded his head and jumped from the bed.

"Let's get a chair." Joseph said. When Adam had climbed the thin round rungs and stood on the wood seat in front of the lower part of the mirror Joseph handed him the comb.

"You do a good job."

"Mama showed me."

"Did your mama bring you through the woods?"

Adam shook his head. "She died."

"How did you find us by yourself and in the dark?"

"Mr. Smith told me to run. I did until I couldn't. Then I sat down." He handed the comb back. "Your dogs scared me when they barked."

"Was your father with you?"

He shook his head. "Just Mr. and Mrs. Smith. Papa was killed by a frightened horse. That's when mama got sick."

"What was she sick from?"

"Heart sick, Mrs. Gavitt called it, 'cause she missed papa." He was quiet for a moment. Tears welled in his eyes.

"Would you like to help in the shed this morning?"

Adam nodded, brushing away the tears.

"Let's have something to eat first," Joseph said as he uncovered the bread and butter on the cabinet. "And, I'll get some milk," he said as he went to the lid-covered crock inside the outdoor lean-to.

"What would you like to help with in the barn?" Joseph asked between bites of soft bread.

"Milk Bessie?"

"If she's agreeable," he said, laughter in his voice.

As he ate, Adam's eyes settled on the far corner of the log cabin, away from the fireplace and across from their sleeping area. Several chair-high stumps formed a work area. Tools hung on the log cabin wall. The plow Joseph had finished sharpening stood there. Stacked on the floor were bowls and plates which had been rounded out of wood chunks. Eating utensils, carefully whittled, lay beside several newly made handles for farm tools.

In the dim light from the table lantern and from the fireplace, Trudy and Joseph had cracked nuts of hickory and walnuts, storing the nutmeats in crocks for later use.

"Where's Trudy?" Adam asked as he set his empty cup down.

"Trudy's a midwife." Joseph answered. "While you were asleep a neighbor came by to pick her up. She helps babies to be born."

"Mrs. Gavitt helped mama when I was born."

That afternoon Joseph and Adam struggled to roll a three-foot-long log that measured four feet in diameter, to get it inside the shed door. Most of the four-foot section Joseph had already hollowed out with an ax.

Finally when it was inside, Joseph sat down heavily, his face red from exertion. "Whew, it was harder to move than I thought it would be."

"Why do you want this?" Adam asked.

"Trudy wants a tub to take a bath in, and to wash our clothes in. This should do, don't you think?"

Adam looked puzzled.

Joseph laughed out loud and again affectionately mussed up Adam's blond hair. "Doesn't look like a tub does it?"

"No," answered Adam honestly.

"It will," Joseph said smiling. He picked up his hammer and wood chisel.

Starting about two inches from the edge where the bark had been, he began chipping out small chunks of wood. "It'll take a lot of time and work to get this chipped all the way around and almost to the bottom. When that's done, it'll need to be smoothed out so no one gets splinters."

Adam looked doubtful.

Easily reading Adam's face, Joseph grinned, "One day soon it will be Trudy's tub," he said.

Early the next morning the dogs barked, issuing an alarm. Joseph awoke instantly and quickly crawled over the sleeping boy.

He was out of bed, across the room, reaching for his gun when he heard Trudy's familiar voice calming the dogs. He put the gun back on the rack and unlocked the door to see Trudy heading towards the cabin. Though the trees were almost bare of leaves, the early light barely trickled through to the forest floor. In the dim natural light and with the glow of a lantern, Trudy had been escorted home.

Though dreary, the heavy air outside was calm. "It's hard to breathe in the woods today. The air is so close." Trudy said by way of greeting him. Once in the house she took off her coat and boots. Standing in front of Joseph she kissed him soundly and hugged him tightly.

"I missed you!" she said and kissed him again.

"And we missed you," he said tilting her chin upwards and giving her a soft kiss.

For a while they stood holding hands watching Adam as he slept. Then Joseph went to the chest and opened the top drawer pulling out the papers. Hearing the rustle, Trudy turned. Involuntarily her hand covered her mouth.

"Come," Joseph said gently taking her hand away from her mouth. He led her to the table. After lighting the wick of the lamp he carefully put the globe over it. When both were seated, he turned over the first sheet of paper. It was Adam's baptismal certificate. The boy is the issue of Freda and Henry Miller of Maumee, Ohio.

"My sister's boy," Trudy said her voice barely a whisper.

"He has your blonde hair, that's for sure," Joseph said as he turned over the second sheet.

"Their marriage certificate," Trudy said, "but why did they send Adam and those papers to us?" She looked at the marriage certificate again. "Look," she pointed, "there are our signatures as witness to their marriage.

Trudy's hand flew to pick up the sealed, folded sheet and tore it open. Two small cards fell onto the table. She turned them over. "Ohhh.... They're funeral cards...of Freda and of Henry. Joseph, how can that be?" She questioned and then trembling, "there must be a mistake."

"Adam told me his parents were both gone," Joseph said quietly, as he put his arms around her. For a moment, he held her, then turned back to the last sheet still face down on the table.

He turned it over. A letter detailed the circumstances of Adam's coming to them. It said that he was traveling with an Alvira and Christopher Smith, "who are from good families and want to settle in the wilderness." In return for the Smiths escorting Adam, the writer asked that Joseph and Trudy help the couple get settled.

At the very bottom of the letter was a note about some monies due Adam. They were to inquire at the address listed. The letter was signed by a solicitor, who they both knew as being a partner to Henry, Freda's husband.

Involuntarily her hand and then her whole body began to shake. Minutes passed before a tear trickled down Trudy's face, followed by a burst of heart rending sobs that she buried in Joseph's shoulder.

Joseph, white-faced and shaken, held her until the first spasms of her emotional pain ceased. Then he went to the fireplace and put a log on the fire to heat water to make tea. From the bench beside the fireplace he brought a quilt and wrapped it around Trudy's shoulders. He helped her to the rocker and placed a short stool under her feet. He sat beside her on a chair and held her hand until the water was hot enough for the tea.

Silent hours slipped away as Adam slept and they reconciled themselves to their pain. Later still, for lack of someway to comfort his wife, Joseph told her about the tub that he and Adam had brought into the shed.

"When it is done, I will make our boy a bed of his own." Leaning over he kissed her tenderly.

PART TWO

Thirteen Years Later
September 1838

CHAPTER 1
Canal Prices

"Only twelve-and-a-half cents a bushel for all our hard work," Adam said impatiently and angrily. "If we could sell this corn along the canal we'd get thirty-five cents. A bushel of our potatoes would bring us forty cents, not nineteen cents like we got yesterday in Schinbone."

"Those are canal prices, not our selling prices," Joseph said, trying to reason with Adam. "When the canal is through here, we'll get those better prices."

"We can at least take what we have left and sell it at the warehouses in Piqua."

"Getting there and returning is still dangerous; besides I can't leave for that long."

"I'll go," Adam said. "Jake and Zach would go with me."

"They're your neighbors and friends, Adam. It's dangerous for all of you," said Trudy.

"We'll be careful, Aunt Trudy, and we'll take our guns."

Trudy and Joseph both agreed that Adam and his close friends were all too young to make the trip. But Adam's mind was made up.

When the harvest was finished at mid-September, though Trudy was worried about Adam and his friends, she hugged him. "Stay safe," she said, her concern evident in her eyes. He would never be old enough in her mind, but he was physically old enough, as were his friends, to decide what they would do with their lives.

The trio left on the farm wagon at barely dawn. Following the dirt road, by mid-morning they were at the summit between St. Marys and Berlin at a town called New Bremen. There was much hustle and bustle as the excavation for the canal had started here. Trees were being felled by many men, and teams of horses helped to clear away the long timbers.

From this point, the canal was to go both north and south. They were on a plateau in the southern-most place on the North American Continental Divide. From there the water flowed north.

Huge numbers of men, around 500, were working from the center of the town, going in both directions. Adam and his friends watched. They had expected to see a canal already finished, but were seeing only the start of one being dug. It was a huge labor in process.

"Some day this canal will reach all the way from Cincinnati to Lake Erie," one of the local men said. The three travelers believed it was possible, but also knew it would take an almost inhuman effort in labor.

Hours later Adam walked with Zachariah on the dim, dirt path in front of the large workhorse and farm wagon. Half asleep, Jake swayed on the seat, the reins loose in his hands. The narrow road was thick with trees, brush and small animals. They passed by the fortress of Berlin and continued on.

Adam and Zach carried their guns as they walked.

"That's more oak than hickory," said Adam.

"And more squirrels than rabbits," Zach answered. "Score's even."

The snapping of a branch immediately alarmed Adam. Before he could turn, a buckskin-clad bandit jumped him; another attacked Zach.

Both Adam and Zach moved fast. They were fighting for their lives when they heard the shot.

The two bandits they fought heard it, too, immediately making for the forest. As Adam got his bearings he saw another bandit run from the back of the farm wagon into the forest. It was then that Adam realized it'd been his gun that had gone off in the midst of the scuffle.

He and Zach ran to Jake, who had fallen back on top of two wooden barrels, already partially covered with Jake's blood. He lay on the full bed of the wagon, blood gushing from his thigh.

Together Adam and Zach climbed in beside their friend. "We're here," Zach said.

Quickly they moved stacks of leather strap-bound, soft furs and pelts, arranging them to make a bed. On top they threw their woolen blankets and moved Jake to this cushion.

Within moments Adam was driving the farm wagon as fast as the workhorse would move. Behind him Zach pulled off his own shirt and ripped it into sections. He soaked up the blood on Jake's thigh. By pressing hard against the wound he was able to nearly stop the bleeding. "We need to find help soon," he said loud enough for Adam to hear over the clip clopping of the horse's heavy feet and the creaking farm wagon.

Adam nodded his head and slapped the reins on the horse's back. His stomach felt jittery. He gripped the reins tightly to keep his hands from shaking. "Giddy-up," he said, and slapped the reins on the rump of the horse once more.

Maybe I am too young, he thought. Automatically his hand went to the jagged scar on the bottom of his chin. Memory of how he'd gotten that scar flashed through his mind.

This was my idea. Again the memory. It had been his idea that time, too. He'd told his Uncle Joseph that he could ride the work horse. Even though his uncle told him not to, he was sure he could, and did, until he slipped off and hit his chin on that rough rock, leaving him a scar. *This is more serious. If he dies it'll be my fault.*

"There's a house," yelled Zach as they rounded a bend in the path, "Ahead of us, in that clearing."

"There's a child, too." Adam said loudly pointing toward the back of the clapboard house. "They have to help us!" A barn and another small out-building shared the landscape.

"Let's hope they know about gun shot wounds." Zach said.

"Gee," Adam commanded pulling on the right rein leading the horse into the turn.

The child was a young girl, who now stood at the side of the house staring at the rattling, rolling wagon coming toward her, hitting potholes in the pathway.

Adam asked quickly, "Is your Pa around?" She shook her head. "Is your Ma here?" They had come to a stop. She opened her mouth to answer just as a man several years older than Adam came out of the house.

Zach, near panic, said in an overly loud voice, "Can you help us? Jake's been shot."

In seconds the situation registered in the man's mind. Immediately he looked at the farm wagon. He was tall and lanky and talking to someone inside the doorway. "A man's been shot, Ma." Then he jumped from the porch and ran toward the wagon.

Adam tied the reins to the brake and jumped from the farm wagon as the man came up beside them. "We were attacked. Jake got shot," he said. He reached out his hand. "My name's Adam Miller."

"Bring him in," said the woman now on the porch of the house.

"Call me Natt." the man said, quickly shaking Adam's hand.

Zach reached for the two corners of the blanket nearest Jake's head. "Let's use this to move him."

"That'll work," Natt agreed, his black, unruly hair falling in his face. He grabbed one corner of the blanket. Adam grasped the other. Together they carried Jake up the steps into the three-room house.

They passed the girl who made neither a sound, nor a movement, only watched. Her long colorless dress, stained and dirt smudged, hung limply, as did her dark straggly hair.

"Put him on the table," the woman said. Carefully they took him from the blanket and laid him on the bare wood table. "Move away so I can take a look at him. Her voice was soft, but not without purpose. Her clean blue dress was faded. She secured her dark graying hair in a bun. Her light gray eyes, like her voice, were soft and looked bright and kind.

"Can you help him, do you know about gun shot wounds?" Zach asked, his sentences cutoff, his voice shaky.

She nodded her head. "Looked after them afore," In the same breath she directed Natt, "Bring me a clean, hot rag," while she covered herself with an apron. From the apron pocket she pulled out small sharp shears and began cutting Jake's pant leg. Quietly she talked to Natt. "Put my knife and tweezers in that pan of hot water."

"Can you hold him steady while I look at this?" she asked Zach.

"Yes, ma'am."

An hour later, Jake was asleep. The wound was clean and had stopped bleeding. She had bandaged it with strips from a clean sheet.

"Put him on that bed over there," she said as she wiped her hands on a clean rag. "He's lost a lot of blood but I think he'll live."

"Thank you, ma'am," Zach said, tears welling in his eyes.

"You're welcome, son. That's why we're put here," she said, "to help each other." She patted him on the shoulder. "Now the two of you sit for a spell."

She looked at Natt as he cleaned the table with a hot, wet towel.

"Thank you," she said. "I'll finish." She took the towel from him. "Will you saddle up Wind and go find the Doc? Ask him to stop out here and take a look at this boy?"

Natt nodded, ran his hand through his hair combing it in place, and quietly left the house.

CHAPTER 2
Leaving a Friend

Adam sat up straight on the makeshift bed of straw he and Zach shared inside the barn. He watched as shadows of lantern light filtered through the barn siding. Someone was coming.

Natt, lantern in hand, opened the door and led Wind inside. He nodded to Adam in greeting, and looked at Zach who slept soundly. Setting the lantern on the dirt floor, he proceeded to ready Wind for his stall.

"Did you find the Doc?" Adam asked.

"It took some, but I did. He'll be out in the morning." Natt closed the stall door and turned to rub Wind's nose. "Doc said with Ma doing the mending we more'n likely don't need to worry."

Adam breathed a sigh of relief. Not until then did he realize how tense he was. He opened his mouth to speak, but, nothing came out. Instead he cleared his throat. Finally, when he was able, "God was with us in finding you," he said.

Natt nodded.

"Your Ma was a life-saver for us."

"She helped with the wounded in a militia company coming south from fighting in Michigan territory." For a moment he fidgeted, looking down at the floor. "She's not really my Ma."

"How come you call her Ma then?"

"She's took care of me since I was five." He hunkered down next to Adam. "My folks were killed by renegade Indians." He picked at a long piece of straw, sticking one end of it in his mouth. He chewed on it as he talked. "She always tells me that when she saw me she knew she needed to keep me.... Was the same with Nellie. Her folks just left her off one day and kept on going. Nellie's a little strange because of it."

"How old is she?"

"We guess about six. She's been here since early spring." Natt took the straw out of his mouth. "She'll be better, in time."

Zach in his sleep, turned over on his stomach.

"He's worn out," Adam said. "We're farmers. We don't do much traveling. For sure we've never been attacked before."

"You on your way to sell your load?"

Adam nodded. "Heading to Piqua, hoping for better prices."

"You'll get them. You can be sure of that. I've thought of going there again to take some extra corn we have."

"Be glad to have you come with us."

"We'd be safer together," Natt said considering it. "I'll talk to Ma."

"Isn't your Pa around?"

He's an Indian agent. Out working for the Federal Government at the northern reservations. Trying to get the remaining Indians to leave Ohio and move West."

For a moment there was an awkward silence.

"How long will it take us to get to Piqua from here?"

"Another full day for sure, with your farm wagon and workhorse."

"We're slow but this is all we have. Do you think your Ma would be agreeable to keeping Jake?"

"'Til he's better, Ma won't let him out of her sight." Natt stood up. "I'll talk to her when I get in. Let's plan to start early." Taking a step backward he picked up the lantern. "See you at dawn."

"Nite," Adam said, laying back down on their bed of straw. He put his hand behind his head, thinking over the situation with Jake.

His train of thought ran to the next day and to the canal. He'd talked to everyone he knew who'd seen the canal. Still he couldn't imagine what this canal was going to look like. His mind wandered, going back to that morning when they passed through New Bremen where stones for the 90-foot-long canal locks were just being gathered. His mind questioned what he'd read. *They call it a big ditch, but how big? The size of a river, a creek?* He rolled over to sleep, his last thought, *By tomorrow I'll know.*

CHAPTER 3
A Canal

They'd traveled for over half of a day and had seen few other people. The pathway gradually had become wider, and the trees by degrees were cut further away from the dirt road. The widened ruts were deeper on the hardened ground.

"Looks like we're gett'n close to Piqua," Natt said.

"I thought we had a ways to go," Adam said perking up from the tiresome journey.

"Still a half day's ride," Natt said. "We'll have to pull over by dusk and get a full night's sleep."

"I'd hoped to see the canal today," the disappointment sounded in Adam's voice.

"Me, too," said Zach.

The next morning they awoke when the early light was still dim. Within minutes they put their feet inside of their boots, brushed down their hair, and dusted off their clothes. After rolling up their blankets each found seating on the wagon. As they rode they chewed on biscuits Ma had given to Natt. Fall was in the air, and the three were rare'n to go.

An hour later in the full light of the morning they saw the Miami River. Along it was the canal. Adam pulled the horse reins tight, stopped the horse, and stared at the forty-foot wide ditch running alongside the river.

As they watched, the quiet waters of the canal began to ripple. A boat, painted in bright hues of blue and yellow, slowly moved on the water as two mules on the towpath pulled it. Hitched in tandem, they were driven on the ten-foot wide towpath by a young lad of about twelve who sat on one of the mules.

All around silence prevailed except for the light lap of the water on the sides of the boat, a snort or two from the mules, and the urging commands from the boy controlling them. The three men were engulfed by the lazy mood as they watched the slow, even movement of the boat loaded with cord wood and stone. It passed by and was barely out of sight when another boat followed. This one, nearly 80 feet long and at least 12 feet wide, was painted white. In dark blue letters on the front the name **Last Chance** was printed. Horizontal stripes of the same dark blue were painted on the white cabin.

A rattling wagon hauling produce pulled up behind their wagon, drawing their attention away from the boat. It forced Adam to move on further down the dirt road that followed the canal. As soon as Adam could, he stopped the wagon to look again. They watched as another boat on the canal came to a dead stop.

"What's going on here?" Zach asked. He looked puzzled, scratching the back of his head.

"I don't know," Adam answered.

"There's a turn-around basin and then there's a lock."

"What's a turn-around basin?" Zach asked.

"A place where boats can be repaired, or just turn around to go in the other direction. Then there is the lock, too," said Natt.

"The lock is what they were collecting stones for in New Bremen," Adam said. "How does a lock work?"

They walked to the canal edge. "From here," Natt said, "you can see two wooden gates at the end of the two stone walls ahead. That gate is open now but it'll swing closed. There's one on the other end, it will close too. When those gates are closed Lock 9 of Piqua is water-tight.

"Let's watch the boat go in," said Natt. "See that piece of timber up on the top of the lock walls? It's used as the handle of a lever. They call it a sweep. The lock-keeper pushes it one way and the gate opens," Natt explained. "When he pushes it the other way the gate closes."

They watched the mules on the path walk to the side of the wall and further ahead of the lock until the boat was inside the narrow walls. Then the lock keeper closed the gates on both ends.
"Now what happens?" Zach asked.

"There are small openings called sluice gates below the lock gates. When they are open water can either come in or go out of the lock," Natt said.

"And the water level goes up or down depending on whether the boat is to go up or down. Right?" asked Adam.

Natt nodded. "That's how it works," he said.

They watched until the boat was quietly pulled onward out of the lock. For a moment the wide expanse of water that ran only yards from the Miami River was still again.

"Natt, were you here when they dug this part of the canal?" Adam asked.

He nodded.

"What's a feeder?" asked Zach now quite interested in the canal setup and having heard the term.

"It's a short canal which branches off the main canal. Feeders are constructed to bring water into the canal and sometimes dug to reach small towns that are not on the main canal." He made a motion to indicate the main canal in front of them. "This is not a feeder."

Turning to point out the Miami River beside the canal he said, "The water source for the canal here is the river. At different areas of the main canal there are other water sources. The river also has gates. The canal butts up against them. The gates are opened or closed depending on whether or not the canal needs water to keep boats afloat."

They followed in the wagon on a road close to the towpath by the canal, to the town of Piqua, where there was more activity. Adam and Zach turned their heads, first one way and then the other, trying to take in everything at once.

"I think you'd better give me the reins," Natt said, "so you can have a better look."

"Good idea," Adam said handing the reins to Natt.

"Look!" Zach said pointing to a group of men near the edge of the canal placing planks on the side of a stopped canal boat. Two men rolled huge barrels down the planks. Others lifted bags of grain onto their shoulders and then carried them down to the boat.

Earlier the work horse had taken them toward the road by the buildings along the canal. Now Natt urged the workhorse to move even closer.

When I tell Uncle Joseph about all this maybe he'll be more agreeable to making this trip himself, Adam thought. Remembering the attack, and how badly Jake was hurt Adam also wondered if his uncle might possibly never agree to come.

CHAPTER 4
The Market

The late September afternoon sun beat down hot on the town's tall, narrow, wood and brick buildings that sat close to the canal bed. Slight shadows were cast along the dirt street between the canal and the rear entrances. Here small crowds milled about.

Potatoes by the bushel or by the piece, cabbages, turnips, and sweet potatoes were being sold on or beside vendors' stands. Some stands were only a board on top of two barrels; others were two-wheel carts or crude lean-tos supported by strong branches. New pottery plates, cups, bowls, forks and spoons coming from Cincinnati were displayed. Sharp kitchen knives, long-handled sickle blades, prongs and iron rods to poke fires, baskets and many other items were all for sale.

In another area, lines of carts, wagons, and a few sleds formed near the warehouses of the merchants who were buying and giving directions, pointing and shouting to the farmers and traders, telling them which warehouse or area to unload their cargo.

Contagious excitement was in the air, and Adam prepared to take their turn at dickering with a merchant for their product's best price.

Those who'd made their sales walked slowly, but with determination back to unload their transports. The eyes of all looked tired.

Natt pulled the buckboard slowly ahead, his excitement building.

"Which line should we get in?" Adam asked. Zach leaned forward to hear the answer.

"It's your load," Natt said.

"You decide, Natt." Then with a grin on his face he looked at the lines and said, "Who would have thought we'd have a choice." Turning to Natt he said, "It's a good thing you're with us."

"Let's get behind that wagon," Natt said slapping the reins lightly to move the horse on.

"Either of you any good at trading?" Natt asked.

"I've never done it," Zach said.

"We'll let you do the dickering," Adam said. "You know how these men think."

"I've done some," Natt said rather proud of his experience. "I'll do my best."

As the rays of sunshine squeezed between the buildings, Nat haggled with the merchant. Both walked around the wagon checking the quality and condition of the goods. The merchant looked intensely at Adam and Zach. Finally, as though he was satisfied, he settled on a price and began peeling off bills from a roll he kept in his trousers' pocket. From a small bag that he also carried he handed Natt a handful of silver coins.

"Divide this between yourselves. My runner will ride with you to make sure you get unloaded at my warehouse." The merchant waved his hand to one of the young boys to jump on the back of the wagon.

Natt put the money in his pocket, got up on the farm wagon, and picked up the reins. The runner yelled directions.

"Giddy up." Natt said, smacking the reins on the rump of their workhorse. They followed a well-worn path. On their right, on a more narrow stretch of road, they saw a one-story brick building. Swinging doors opened the full length of the building. As they passed, a boom swung out through an opening. It reached out far enough to load or unload a canal boat docked at the canal bank.

"Would you look at that!" Zach said staring with his mouth hanging open.

The runner motioned them southward along the canal bank, lining them up behind two other wagons. Inside, the warehouse men were stripped to their waists. Sweat dripped down their foreheads and on their chests as they pushed carts and wheelbarrows, unloading and stacking.

In a short time Natt pulled the wagon up to the warehouse doors. Once unloaded, he lightly slapped the reins on the horse's back, slowly moving the farm wagon away from the warehouse in a southward direction along the side of the canal bank. "Want to see another lock now that we've done what we come for?" Natt asked. "It's only about 300 feet from here."

Adam nodded, and Zach answered, "All right with me."

"We can sit for a spell and then split up the money." Natt hesitated. "We should keep it hidden. It's dangerous having it on us!"

"Where're we gonna hide it?" Adam asked concerned.

"Maybe in your socks. You've got good sturdy boots and woolen socks. Stuff it down in and tie the boot around your ankle."

"Never hid money on myself," Zach said as he reached down to his boot. "Never had much to hide. I guess it'll fit there."

Later Natt stopped the buckboard again and pointed toward the lock. "There it is!"

A canal boat was in the process of making its way in between the narrow space of the stone walls. The mules stopped on the path. Boatmen were using long poles to line up the boat in the narrow confines of the ninety-foot-long walls of the lock.

"All clear," a boatman yelled.

The lockkeeper, who stood on top of the lock itself, shoved on the long-handled plank to sweep the gate closed behind the boat. Rushing, he covered the space between the back of the boat to the front. Taking hold of the other sweep-handle, he closed the gate in front of the boat, boxing it in.

He then pulled a lever which lifted the lid to the wicket or sluice gate. Water poured out from under the boat until the water level in the lock was the same as the water level (five or six feet) in the lower section of the canal. The lockkeeper then unboxed the boat by opening the wooden gate in front of it, and the boat was on its way again in less than a half-hour.

Adam's imagination carried him away as he watched the two mules, harnessed in tandem, pull their load. He could almost experience the floating sensation himself. *What a grand feeling,* he thought.

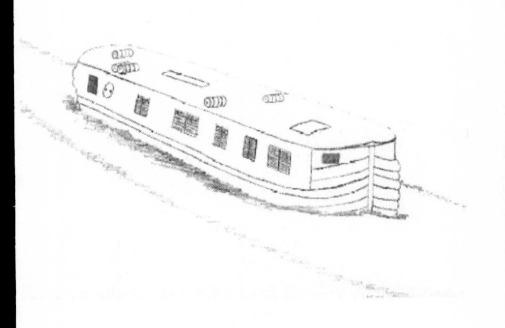

Passenger Boat

CHAPTER 5
Diversions

Back in the village, because of the din of voices, they hadn't been able to hear the clip clop of their horse's hooves, but now they could.

In one day the three men had finished all their business and entered a new and exciting world. Adam's mind reeled with all the possibilities opening up as they rode back to the market in silence. Quite suddenly, Natt pulled tight on the reins, jerking the wagon to a stop. "Let's walk around a bit before we head back," he said. He nodded and raised an eyebrow toward a well endowed, dark haired girl. Flirtatiously, he winked at her.

"Let's do," they readily agreed. All three jumped from their seats at a nearby hitching post.

Adam casually tied the reins. Carefully, Natt ran his fingers through his thick, unruly, dark hair, and grinned at Adam and Zach. Quickly he was off in the direction of the young woman.

Zach nudged Adam, "suppose he knows that girl?"

Adam grinned. "Could be," he said as he and Zach walked.

Zach, unusually quiet, suddenly spoke. "What do you think of Annie?"

"Annie Schmidt?" Adam asked.

"Yeah."

"I've known her for years. Have you taken a fancy to her?" Adam asked.

"Think I like her…but I've never spoken to her about it."

"When we get home, go see her."

"Think she'd let me court her?"

"Better talk with her pa."

"What's he like?"

"God fearing and just. You'd better be sure you know what you want."

Zach was again quiet and thoughtful but walked with a little more vigor in his step. The two walked toward the canal. The boat in front of them Natt had called a packet boat. Bright curtains flapped from the inside of its many windows. Quite a good number of traveling passengers had already gotten off of it.

"Let's see if we can get on this passenger boat," Adam said as they got close. "I'd like to look at it."

"That man," he pointed toward a tall man dressed in a cap, a pair of dark trousers, and a jacket to match, "seems to be the one in charge." The man looked around as though he was readying himself to get off the boat.

Adam led, walking faster, wanting to intercept the man. Misjudging the distance the man covered with his long legs, the two nearly collided. At a disadvantage, Adam found it difficult to speak. "SSSorry sir," he blurted, embarrassed, but still determined. "Are you the Captain?" He looked up at the man whose brown hair curled over the edge of his cap.

Unruffled he said, "I am. My name's Pohls. Abram Pohls." He held out his hand. "What can I do for you?"

"Adam Miller, sir," he said while reaching out to shake the strong, sun-darkened hand. "My friend Zach Mauer." He nodded in Zach's direction then motioned with his hand toward the boat. "You own it?"

"My two partners and myself," he said.

"Could we take a look around? We've never been on a canal boat.

A smile slowly crossed the man's face. "You're welcome to look around. We leave in an hour. Be off by then." He turned and walked on.

"We'll be off. Thank you, sir," Adam said.

The loud bray of a mule blared behind them, along with heavy clomping footsteps. Two teenage boys in the stable of the boat were struggling with a pair of mules, trying to get them to go up a wooden plank to the towpath.

"Looks like they know it's time to work," Adam said walking to the steps.

"And they don't like the idea!" Zach said.

Both looked into the small narrow stable as the last fresh mule made its way off the boat. The boy left in the stable quickly cleaned up the droppings and wet straw replacing it with dry straw. No sooner had he finished when one of the tired mules willingly and carefully made its way down the plank that had slats of wood nailed every eighteen inches for footholds.

The boy, in cut-off pants, wearing a cap barely covering his head of thick dark hair, pushed the mule to the side of the stable awaiting the other as it started down the plank. Near the end of the plank the second mule stumbled. At the last minute it regained its footing, but not quickly enough to keep from knocking the boy off his feet and losing his cap in the process.

"Look! It's a girl," Zach said.

She looked nervously around.

"A pretty one, at that," said Adam.

"Please don't tell anyone," she said as she got up and moved out of the way of the frightened animal. Hurriedly she stuffed her hair back under the cap.

"Why?" Zach asked.

"Girls aren't allowed to be stable hands on this boat. "Please don't say anything."

"Your secret's safe with us," Adam said. "Anyway, we're just looking, we're not riding." He winked flirtatiously at the grateful girl.

He and Zach turned toward the front of the boat to see what else was on board. They'd taken only a few steps when they heard a moan coming from in front of them. "You'll be all right, pa," a boy of about ten said. "You'll feel better soon."

The older man lay on his stomach stretched across the length of a long flat trunk. His short legs from his knees on stuck out over the end of the trunk nearly touching the side of the boat. His son stood, holding a bucket close to his father's head.

As Adam and Zach got closer they saw the man's eyes were closed. He turned on his side, pulled his legs up, and curled himself into a ball. The boy saw them. "The Captain thinks he's sea sick," the boy said. "He's not. He gets this way on land, too."

"Was he nipping a little too much last night?" Zach asked. "My pa gets like that when he has too much to drink."

"No sir," the boy said, holding the bucket with one hand, and scratching at the mosquito bites on his arm. "We was to Cincinnati to see a Doctor." He fidgeted. "There ain't nothing anyone can do for it." He set the bucket down beside the trunk. "The doctor told him to go back home and learn to live with it. We're on our way home now."

"How much further do you need to go?" Adam asked knowing this was as far as the canal was dug.

"Right here," the boy said, "but Pa can't walk right yet."

"If we help him off where will you go?"

"Home's an hour's walk."

"How about if we put him on our wagon?"

"He might get sick, mister."

"Wagons can be washed down. Ask him if he'd like some help."

The boy leaned over and whispered in his father's ear.

The man's eyes opened, then immediately closed. "I'd be grateful," he said in a quiet, almost delirious voice. He moaned, turning again to his stomach.

"We'll be back," Adam said patting the boy on his shoulder. They went through the passenger and cargo areas, taking the wood steps two at a time as they came off the boat.

"We didn't see much," Zach said.

"Not this time. See if you can find Natt. I'm going for the wagon."

The three men and the farm wagon returned ten minutes later. Adam and Natt hurried down the steps to get the man. Zach followed to help the boy bring up their belongings.

"He feels some better now," the boy said, "his dinner came up."

"Good!" Adam said sitting down beside the man who now stood bracing himself with both of his hands firmly placed on top of the trunk lid. He looked at the boy. "Show Zach which belongings are yours. He'll help you carry them."

Everyone was miserable on the farm wagon. The man's moaning undid their nerves. "There's the house," the boy said, and they all breathed a sigh of relief, but by then the man had finally fallen asleep.

The house stood tall in front of several buildings. Fenced-in fields surrounding the homestead held cattle and horses. "What does your father do?" Adam asked. He looked at the neat, but threadbare clothes worn by the boy and wondered where he fit in.

"Whatever Mr. Charles asks him to do. We can go round by the kitchen," he said motioning for Adam to follow the circle path around to the back of the house.

A middle-aged woman, her brown hair in a bun at the back of her head, waited anxiously for the wagon to stop. Gathering the long skirt of her dress in her hands and hiking it, she ran toward them when she saw her son. "Where's your Pa?"

Then she saw him trying to sit up with a meager smile on his face. "I'm here, Mother, don't worry."

"But we do!" The woman said as she reached a hand toward him. "And Alese has been gone for three days!"

"She'll be back," the boy said to the woman and then introduced her. "My mother."

"Did you see her?" Margaret asked.

"I'll tell you later," he said scratching at the bites he had on his face and arms. "Let's get Pa into the house. These men brought us home from the boat. Pa had a spell."

"Thank you so much," she said and then extended a welcome to them. "We'd like you to stay for supper. Will you?"

Adam looked at Zach and Natt. Both had ravenous appetites and sorely missed home-cooked meals. "Yes, ma'am, if it's not too much trouble."

"We'd like to have you," she said.

"But Mr. Charles..." said Adam.

"Oh pooh!" Margaret said. "He'd be offering if I weren't." She hugged her husband, now able to stand on his own two feet.

Ninety minutes later this same man, Robert, led them into the dining room. His color was beginning to return, but his walk was still a bit wobbly.

As they entered, a portly gentleman, dressed in a suit, vest, tie, and wearing a pocket watch stood at the doorway. "We can't thank you enough for your kindness to Robert and Andrew," he said shaking each of their hands. "This is my wife Elizabeth," he said introducing the woman to his right. "Now, let's eat."

A huge platter of roast beef was set in the middle of the table along with cooked potatoes, chunks of carrots, cabbage, and wedges of fresh tomatoes. Robert held a chair for Mrs. Elizabeth, as Margaret carried in the fresh, sliced bread.

Mr. Charles held up his arm. "Please Margaret, take your apron off. You and your family must join us. There are table settings on the side table. Robert, bring four chairs..." He looked around. "Where's Alese?"

"Here I am," said a girl at the kitchen door. She stood straight, at five-foot-two inches, her tan face framed with dark, heavy hair that fell to her shoulders.

Adam did a double take. *The stable girl...and I am wrong. His eyes met hers. She's not pretty. She's beautiful!*

CHAPTER 6
Infatuated

Adam ate his food, hardly tasting it, seeing only the girl who sat across from him.

"Robert," Mr. Charles asked, "Did you hear what the price of corn and potatoes was in Cincinnati this morning before you left?"

"No sir, I didn't. We were in a hurry to get on the boat, and then I didn't feel very well."

"It'll be in the Piqua newspaper. I'll read it there," Mr. Charles said.

"More than we got today, I'm sure." Adam declared uninvited.

Mr. Charles looked directly at Adam. "You did better today in Piqua than you did at home?"

"Yes sir," Adam agreed. "Thirty-five cents a bushel for each of my four bushels of potatoes." He took a drink from his water glass then added, "We did far better. Last week we got twelve-and-a-half cents a bushel for our corn and nineteen cents a bushel for our potatoes." He paused, "still we've got to get that canal dug through to meet the northern sections."

Zack, busy eating, picked up on the "joining of the northern and southern canal sections" idea. "Will the canal be close to here when they finish the digging?"

"Just a few miles according to the surveys. We're not far from Lockport (later to be called Lockington). There's quite a change in the terrain."

"Isn't that where there's going to be six different locks?" Natt asked.

"Yes," Mr. Charles said.

"Six locks, man alive!" Zach said, imagining the big change in terrain that Mr. Charles mentioned.

"Each lock will take the canal boat to the next water level until it's where the boat can continue on its way," Mr. Charles said.

"Man," Adam said. He stopped eating and placed his knife and fork on his plate. "Digging this canal is hard work! How many men will it take?" he asked. "And how long will it take?"

"You sound personally interested. Are you?" Mr. Charles asked.

"I am," said Adam.

"Good. History is being made now." Mr. Charles said excitedly. "This canal will open up the land between here and Lake Erie."

"Dear," his wife, said. "Let's have some social talk for awhile. We aren't all as interested in the canal as you and these young men."

"You should be, my dear," Mr. Charles said as he turned to her. "I guarantee that some day soon you'll be just as interested as the rest of us." He looked at Robert and changed the subject. "Tell us about your trip south."

"The boat ride was relaxing and very smooth. I liked seeing the farmland along the canal," Robert said, his voice still weak.

"It was great," Andrew said. "But the mosquitoes were so bad I got bites all over me."

Indulgently, allowing Andrew's outburst Mr. Charles turned again to Robert. "What about your impressions of Cincinnati?"

"They're building everywhere. Cincinnati is now a big town. Riverboats cram the docks. There is so much going on."

"What did your doctor say?" Mrs. Elizabeth interrupted.

"My problem is in my ear." His jaw worked as he fought to control his emotions. "The doctor said sometimes these kinds of attacks go away and never come back."

"Then there is reason to hope," said Mrs. Charles.

Slowly Robert shook his head. "Since I've had it for five years he doesn't think that'll happen for me. Says maybe it came from that severe cold I had that bad winter. Or maybe it could be because I'm getting older and that part of my ear is getting worn out," he looked at his wife and then back at Mrs. Elizabeth. "They don't have a name for it, and the doctor said he doesn't see it often in his patients."

"Did he say anything else?"

"That I should get plenty of rest, and not to move around too fast...not much hope in that. He also said that the attacks won't kill me." Resignation told in his voice. "So I have to learn to live with them."

Margaret reached for his hand that rested on the table. "We'll take it one day at a time, dear," she said.

"Thank you, Mother."

"I'm sorry," Mrs. Elizabeth said. "I had such good hopes."

He nodded. "I did, too."

"I've made some of my special grape pie for dessert." Margaret said, getting up from the table. "Alese will you come help me?"

Adam's eyes held the girl in sight until the door closed on her small backside.

When the door shut he saw that everyone at the table was watching him.

"She is a fetching young girl," Mr. Charles said.

"That she is," Robert said of his daughter.

Adam felt the heat flush his cheeks as he struggled to keep the conversation going while they ate their dessert. He had to consciously make an effort to keep his mind and eyes off of Alese.

"There is room for the three of you to sleep in the hay loft of the barn tonight," Mr. Charles said.

"Sounds great to me," Natt said. Zach agreed.

To the side, as the others left the room, Mr. Charles asked Adam if he played chess.

"I don't know the game, but I'm pretty good at checkers."

"Good, then checkers it'll be," he said looking at the time on his pocket watch. "Come with me. I'm interested in more of your thoughts about the canal."

Adam followed him to the study where shadows played on the bright-colored, horse-hair plastered walls. Kerosene wall lanterns lit the dark woodwork on the bookcase-lined room. Through the opened windows came a fresh cool breeze.

"Would you care for a bit of peach brandy?" Charles asked as he poured from a decanter into a glass for himself.

"No thanks," Adam answered. "I got sick on it once. I haven't been able to stand the taste of it since."

"Perhaps some apple juice?"

"Yes. From your own orchard?"

Mr. Charles nodded. "Now tell me, Adam just why are you so keen on getting this canal built?" He handed him the glass of apple juice.

The two settled in the leather-covered chairs which flanked a small game table. Mr. Charles opened a wooden box he'd taken from the book-lined wall and placed the chessmen that had been on the table inside the black box. "There are checkers in the drawer on your side of the table."

"Red or black?" Adam asked, taking the checkers from the box.

"I'll take red," Mr. Charles answered placing the chessmen back in the bookcase.

The board set up, Charles started the game by quickly putting one of his men out in front of his line. Adam followed suit, his man matching Mr. Charles'. For a few minutes they sparred until Mr. Charles relaxed and picked up his brandy. "Do you think digging the canal is as hard work as farming?"

"Looks like it to me; maybe even harder."

"What are your thoughts on the canal?"

"I've heard a lot about the canal, still I look at it as a farmer sees it," Adam said.

"You're a farmer by trade then?"

"You might say by trade," Adam answered. "My parents are dead. My Aunt and Uncle raised me, and they're farmers. So I've come by it naturally, though my father was a solicitor."

"Do you like farming?"

"I've never done anything else. It's not an easy way to make a living and not very profitable." He paused, "That's why we need the canal."

"I can't argue that."

Adam crowned a king for himself. "It looks like that's the only way we're going to get ahead."

"I think you're right about that too," Mr. Charles said, crowning a king. "I'm interested in the canal, but from a different aspect."

"How so?"

"Land values."

Adam won the first game and reset the checkers. This time, he took the first turn. "Land values of farm lands?" he questioned.

"Not necessarily, but that, too. A few years back when I had a little extra cash I bought some land up north. I wasn't aware of a swamp being anywhere near, but I've learned since, that is where the land I purchased is located."

"What would the canal do for your land?"

"If it goes through where the engineers plan, it would help drain the area, and make me some good money. Not great, but good money. At the very least I'd get my investment back."

"Why do you want to know what I think?"

"When the canal was first talked about, quite awhile before I bought that land, I thought the idea of the canal was crazy. Just a bunch of fools, wanting to spend our government's money," Mr. Charles said. "It's not even finished, and already land values from here to Cincinnati have increased tremendously. "Mr. Charles' king jumped Adam's last king. The second game went to Mr. Charles. "You up to a third?" he asked Adam.

"Certainly," Adam answered with a smile. "Someone has to break the tie."

This time Mr. Charles moved his man first.

"How interested are you in building the canal?"

"I want it to go through."

"Do you want to join the workers? Make enough money to buy your own farm?"

"I never considered that. It would help to make sure it gets built."

"You're only one man. Do you want to work that hard?"

Adam shook his head.

"I know a few people."

"What do you mean?"

Mr. Charles became serious. "Check out the canal-building business. See what you think about it and where you might be able to help with it. If you find something you'd like to do, get back to me."

"Get back to you? Why?"

"Maybe if our minds end up on the same track we might be able to get something accomplished. As I said, I know some important people in the state. Sometimes that can be a big help." Mr. Charles adjusted his seating to a more comfortable position. "Besides, you helped me by bringing Robert and Andrew home. I'd like to help you." He looked directly at Adam. You think about it, and then send me a note or come see me when you've decided."

"I can do that," Adam said as he crowned the first of his men.

Mr. Charles, in like, crowned his first king. For a few minutes they played seriously. Being closely matched, they enjoyed a fast-moving game. It was so close, that Adam knew he could take the last of Mr. Charles' men, but calculating his moves carefully, he placed one of his men in danger's way and Mr. Charles won.

"That was a tight game," Mr. Charles said, a wide smile on his face. "I enjoyed the challenge. Next time you're around and you have the time maybe I'll teach you that chess game."

"Looks like maybe I still need some pointers on my checker game," Adam said affably, stifling a yawn. "It's been a long few days. If you don't mind, I'd like to turn in."

"Certainly," Mr. Charles said and led the way to the door, giving directions on how to get outside.

Adam walked quietly through the dim hallway to the door that opened out to the garden. In the moonlight he could see the outline of the barn. Also, in the moonlight the dying summer flowers were visible. Looking carefully he saw colorful daisies, ferns and ivy lining both sides of the flag-stone walk. Behind those were others ready to drop their seeds and some needing to be dug before winter. He wondered who would do the digging, when suddenly from behind he was bumped.

"Oh," Alese stepped back after nearly knocking him down. "I'm sorry," she said putting her hand out to help him catch his balance.

"I was looking at your flowers," he said. "My aunt would like to see these in full bloom."

"They were so pretty this summer."

"They still are," Adam said.

"Mr. Miller, I want to thank you again for not telling the Captain about me this afternoon."

"You're welcome, Miss Reed," he said noticing again the dress she was wearing. *Much more feminine than the pants she wore on the boat,* he thought. He felt the rush of blood to his face.

"It was very kind of you to bring Father and Andrew home."

"They would have done the same." He shifted his weight, grasping for something to say. "Do you work as a stable girl often?"

"As often as I can. I intend to earn enough money to go to the new Oberlin College to learn accounting. They accept girls, you know."

"Why would a pretty girl like you want to do that?" He swallowed hard, embarrassed by his own words, yet he was puzzled. "You could marry any man you set your mind to, and he'd gladly take care of you!"

"You're too generous, Mr. Miller." She looked down at her toes, barely visible from under the long dress.

"Call me Adam."

"If you call me Alese," she said shyly. "I could marry, but I…don't want someone else to take care of me all my life." She paused a moment. "When I look at Mother and Father, I wonder what will become of them if something happens to Mr. Charles and Mrs. Elizabeth. My parents never worked for anyone else. What will they do; where will they go?" Her voice rose in emotion as she spoke. "And Father is not well."

Adam suddenly felt the need to put his arms around her and hold her, but with effort, refrained himself. "Do your parents know what you do when you're away from the house?"

"Mother doesn't. Andrew knows, and I think Father suspects. He understands, but Mother would worry herself to death, so I can't tell her."

"Do they know you want to go to school?"

She looked up at him. "Mother does. She's talked to Father about it. There is no way. They don't have the money." With determination she added, "I'll do it on my own if I must."

"You've got to be careful," Adam said, definitely not liking the thought of her being in danger. "Isn't there anything else you can do to earn the money?"

She lowered her head again. "I haven't been able to come up with anything and neither has Mother." She looked up then, intently inquiring of him. "I don't remember seeing you around Piqua. Have you been here before?"

"This is the first time, but I think I will be coming this way again."

She clasped her hands behind her, looking like a young schoolgirl. "I'd like that," she said.

"I would too," he said. He could hardly tell her differently. From the moment he saw her at the kitchen door before supper he'd had trouble pushing her from his mind. Not that he had wanted to, but there were other things he needed to think about.

They walked slowly to the garden gate. Reluctantly he reached to pull back the latch. Turning around he looked at her. She was so beautiful. Leaving her standing there was not what he wanted to do; still...he had to get up early. "I'm sure I'll be coming back soon," he said, by way of saying good night.

"I'll look forward to that," she said looking into his eyes.

He could feel his blood rush as once again he turned. This time he left through the open gate.

In the morning Adam greeted Andrew, who ran out to the barn with a basket filled with breakfast biscuits and a jar of strawberry jam.

"Ma says this is for the three of you." In another package under his arm she sent fruit and a fresh loaf of bread. He repeated his mother's words. "'For the trip home,' she said."

"Thank you, Andrew. We'll leave the basket after we eat the biscuits."

"Can I talk to you?" the boy asked.

"Sure you can. What is it?"

"Thank you for helping me with Pa."

"You're welcome," Adam said as he ruffled Andrew's brown hair.

"You're coming back soon?"

"I'm not sure how soon, but I do intend to come back." Inside his heart he wanted to see Alese again and perhaps Mr. Charles.

"Bye. I gotta go help Pa," Andrew said.

The air was cool, the grass damp as the three prepared to get on the farm wagon behind the workhorse. Moments later they were ready to pull out of the drive with Adam handling the reins.

One last time he looked up toward the house which stood quiet this early in the morning. A sheer curtain on the second floor moved slightly, but enough that he could see Alese looking down at them as they drove on. *She's interested,* he thought.

CHAPTER 7
Nellie

For a full day the tired men rode on the wagon as the workhorse plodded toward home. After stopping early for the night and eating their small evening meal around the campfire they loosened their bed rolls and turned in, each arranging himself close enough to the fire to feel its warmth yet far enough away that sparks spitting from it would not burn their blankets.

For the middle of September the evenings were cool, the days still very warm, almost hot. The next day was not different as they drove toward Natt's home where Jake was staying. A horse-pulled carriage, its windows draped in black fabric, passed the slower moving wagon. Natt's family home was still not within eyesight. From a side path another carriage, with dark colored curtains drawn, pulled in front of them.

"Do you know them?" Adam asked Natt.

"I couldn't say for sure, but it looked like the local preacher." A clouded look passed over his eyes. "Someone must have died."

Now within sight of Natt's home they saw the first carriage turn into his driveway. While still behind the second carriage, they saw another horse-drawn carriage, its windows also draped, coming from the other direction, follow the first carriage into the driveway.

"My God!" was all that Natt said as he jumped from the wagon and ran ahead, whizzing past the carriage in front of them. Little dust clouds rose behind his heels.

Adam and Zach looked at each other. "Jake!" they said in unison. Adam, frightened and impatient, whipped the reins on the back of the big workhorse. The farm wagon pulled in behind the last of the carriages.

Jake stood on the porch leaning on a cane. Though he didn't smile he looked pleased to see them and slowly made his way over to the steps to greet them. Past the wave of relief, though still full of concern, they walked toward him. Natt was nowhere in sight. People from the carriages were gathering in the back yard.

With effort Jake made his way down the steps. Adam and Zach met him, not knowing quite what to say.

"You're looking better than when we last saw you." Zach spoke up, walking around Adam to give Jake a hug. "Got yourself a cane, too, I see."

Jake, half proud said, "Indian Pa made it for me."

Adam shook Jake's right hand with both of his and asked quietly, "What's going on here, Natt?"

"Nellie's dead," he said sadly. "She went into the woods like she always did and disappeared for the afternoon. We realized something must be wrong when she didn't return as it started to get dark...." He hung his head. "Wolves got her."

Adam and Zach, stunned, said nothing. Jake added, "Ma found her. She's not taking it well."

"We're sorry," said Adam, unable to bear the hurt look in Jake's eyes. "Is there anything we can do for them?"

"Everything's taken care of," Jake said.

"Is Natt inside with the family?"

"He went directly in when he got here. It has to be an awful shock for him. Nellie was a quiet little girl, but they'll miss her." He pulled a handkerchief from his back pocket to blow his nose.

"What's this?" Adam asked as he looked more carefully at Jake. "You're growing a beard, and a mustache?"

"Yeah," Jake answered. His sadness suddenly seemed to lessen. "How do you like it?" he asked, rubbing his chin.

"It'll take some getting used to," Adam said. "Makes you look a bit like your old Grandpa."

"Oh, come on; it does not!"

"Of course not." He put his arm around Jake's shoulders as he took a deep breath. "Are you sure there isn't something we can help with around here?"

"I think everything is done and they're just about ready." Natt got back just in time."

As they spoke, Indian Pa and Natt came out of the house carrying a small wooden coffin. Natt's Ma followed, wearing a freshly pressed dark dress and a black-veiled hat. Tears stained her face.

"Let me walk with you," Jake said to her as she came down the steps.

"You've been such a help," she said slipping her hand through his arm.

Adam and Zach fell into line behind them until they reached the backyard.

"She was ours only a short time," Indian Pa said. "We're here for her to the end."

He nodded toward the back of the barn as he and Natt carried their burden. The mourners followed quietly. Thirty yards past the barn a short, worn, white wooden fence surrounded two dozen weather-beaten tombstones. The group walked to a small grave site already dug at the far side of the cemetery. There Indian Pa and Natt set the coffin down.

The local preacher said a small prayer finishing with, "Thou art dust, and to dust thou shalt return."

The men bowed their hatless heads. The women dabbed at their eyes with their handkerchiefs.

Natt and Indian Pa, one on each end, picked up the coffin. Two ropes lay across the open grave. Four men from the group took hold of an end of each rope and held it snug as Natt and Indian Pa gently placed the coffin on top. Slowly and evenly the men gave slack to the lengths, lowering Nellie to her final resting place.

Quickly the ropes were pulled from under the coffin and wound into separate coils. The preacher pulled the shovel from the pile of loose dirt, scooped up a shovel full and let it fall on top of the wood coffin. He passed the shovel to Indian Pa, and from there it went to each man. Indian Pa, with graying hair and a round weathered face, stepped back, took his wife by the arm as she laid a bouquet of wild flowers beside the open grave. He gently led her back toward the house.

If we leave early in the morning, Adam thought as they made their way up the porch steps, *we might be able to get home late tomorrow.*

Early the next morning, Ma and Indian Pa, with Natt standing between the two, waved goodbye.

The ride home was slow and tedious. As the miles crept by, Adam wondered if he might get involved with the building of the canal, as Mr. Charles suggested. Or should he remain as he was, only interested in getting the canal finished?

CHAPTER 8
Late October
A Request

A few weeks after they returned home Jake came to visit Adam.

He limped into the barn where Adam sat mending a harness. "Hi," he said, and sat down on a covered wooden box. He passed the time with trivial talk and then said, "My Ma," he hesitated, "wants to ask a favor of you."

Adam looked up from his job. "What does she need?"

"Her brother who lives in Maumee was hurt bad doing road work for the Township. Ma would like to go see him." He moved a bit on the box. "She'd like for you to go with us. She's worried I can't handle things alone yet." He winced as he lifted himself up off the box. "She's probably right."

"Maumee is where I was born," Adam said as he got up. "It'd take a few days to get there."

"We'd take the buggy. It'd take less time and we'll be more comfortable."

"I lived there when I was a small child," Adam said as he hung the harness up on a nail. *Mr. Charles suggested I check out the canal business.* He started to shell corn for the chickens. *This could be just the chance I need.*

"I'll go," Adam said. "I think it might be interesting."

"Great! Ma will be pleased." Jake said heading toward the door. He stopped before going further and looked back at Adam. "We plan to go in two days," he said, "if you can go then."

"I'll be ready."

Late in the afternoon the next day, Adam sat at the table talking with his Aunt Trudy. She handed him the gold watch she'd kept since he was four. "It was my father's," she said, "left to your mother when he died. The Smiths were going to give it to us for safekeeping until you were older." She stood behind him admiring the watch. "I think you are old enough now. You've become a man."

She hugged her nephew from the back. As she did she put a sheet of paper, brown on its edges, its creases somewhat flattened, in front of him. He turned his head to look at her. In his eyes she saw curiosity and trust, as well as his love for her.

"Go ahead, read it," she said. "It's the last of the papers that were sewn into the lining of your coat when you came to stay with us."

"This is the last one, then?" he asked, making sure he'd heard what she said.

"Yes."

He laid the watch down, and one last time Trudy picked it up. He read the letter slowly. When he looked at her next, tears glistened in his eyes. "I came to you as a shock didn't I?"

"Yes, but we desperately wanted you. We love you."

"What is this about monies due me?" He looked at her searchingly. "No one ever said anything about this."

"We're not sure ourselves, but your uncle and I believe it must be your inheritance from your parents."

She placed the pocket watch on the table in front of him.

"That is the gold watch the letter speaks of," she said, "the one you must take with you, along with your baptismal record."

"You want me to claim the monies when I go to Maumee with Jake and his family?"

"It's your decision, Adam. We can no longer make those decisions for you. When you hear what they have to say you'll do what you think is best."

"But I'm not sure I can," he said.

"You will when the time comes. It's in your nature. Your father was a good decision maker, too."

"He couldn't have been that good. He got himself killed and left my mother and me by ourselves!"

"It was an accident, Adam. Accidents happen sometimes to those you love, no matter how careful they might be."

Adam pushed his chair back from the table and ran his hand through his blond hair. He turned the watch over, opened it and closed it several times. "I never counted on an inheritance. You don't know anything about it?" As he spoke he fastened the watch chain to his pants.

She shook her head. "I've got to get the evening meal started," she said and turned her back, leaving him alone with his thoughts.

CHAPTER 9
Family

They were traveling over the half-muddy path-road, carefully trying not to get into any watery sections of land. "We could almost use a boat in some of these areas," Adam said.

"It's a good thing we're starting to have some cold nights," Jake's mother said. "Hopefully it'll freeze, and the ground will be hard when we come back."

They rode along carefully through the sparse daylight of the forest and the stifling close air, all the while swatting at swarms of mosquitoes. "I don't like the cold weather, but I'll be glad to see the frost to get rid of these pests, and to hardened this land," said Jake's mother. "The frost seems late this year."

Adam's hand touched his gun, comforting himself that it was handy if needed. He'd not forgotten those Piqua bandits. Several times he thought he might have seen someone in the shadows of the trees.

Jake, his hands on the reins, told Adam, "We're glad you came with us." Adam, thinking maybe Jake saw something too, picked up his gun. "The thought of more thieves still bothers me," Jake said. He clucked his tongue at the horse and gently slapped its rump with the reins. The horse heard, and feeling the encouragement, increased its gait. Later Adam put his gun down. Storm clouds gathered in the west as they continued northward.

"This is a tough journey," Adam said. "If we have rain, though, the whole trail will be a swamp." Fortunately, without rain, two days later, they reached a road winding along the Maumee River.

"Maybe we should have taken the Maumee Western Turnpike," Jake said.

"Either way it's rough," said Adam, "they're both mud pikes."

They continued on, circumventing numerous near-dry mud holes and by-passing submerged tree stumps in the middle of their path. When the trio set foot in Maumee City they felt relieved.

Jake's family welcomed them as they got out of the buggy. Tears flowed freely and smiles were abundant.

Later, Adam listened to Jake's uncle, Joe. "I'm a cobbler. I've never felled timber, grubbed those aggravating stumps, or graded roads."

"Why were you there?" Adam asked

"Roadwork pays seventy-five cents a day. Our property tax was due. We needed to pay it. Besides, everyone is expected to put in their time working on the roads."

"Exactly how did you get hurt, Uncle Joe?" asked Jake.

"We were using a scraper, pulled by two yoke of oxen, to smooth out the road. The scraper caught on my boot. I lost my balance and fell in between the oxen and the scraper."

"He's lucky to be alive," his wife Edna interrupted. "We can thank God the driver got the oxen stopped before he was killed!" Tears welled in the tired eyes of the older woman. She pulled the edge of her sack-colored apron up and wiped at her tears that melted into the cloth. "I don't know what we'd do without him."

To change the subject Adam asked, "Where is your cobbler shop?"

"It's in the front of the house, Adam. That's why you came in the side door through the kitchen."

Tille, Jake's mother, smiled at her brother. She hadn't seen him since she'd married. "Joe, you're the same good man who stood up for us at our wedding." She got up, walked toward him, stood behind his chair and put her arms around his neck. "I know you're a little older and get tired easier, but brother dear, I still love you." She laid a kiss on his bald head.

"I'm older, all right. I'm a husband and a parent, too." His hearty laugh was cut short when he moved his leg the wrong way and twisted his injured foot. His two little girls ran up to him.

"You all right Papa?" they asked in unison. At five and six they waited on him constantly.

In the kitchen later, Edna started supper, with Tille helping to peel the potatoes.

Everett, Jake's cousin, seemed a bit edgy. "Adam," he asked "Would you mind helping me bring in the wood for the kitchen stove?"

"Be glad to. Need to work off some energy myself," he said, following the twelve-year-old boy out the door.

Jake, enjoying his newfound uncle, was playing a game of checkers with him.

After the large wood box was filled, Adam and Everett brought in fresh drinking and wash water from the well. That evening Everett shared his upstairs bedroom with Adam. The little girls shared their room with Tille. Jake slept on a coverlet laid over the fireplace rug, on the livingroom floor.

Sleep did not come easily to Adam, though he was tired. Worries and doubts about the upcoming visit to see Mr. Waite, the man who had signed the papers he'd carried in his coat as a child, swam in his head.

In the morning, as Adam walked to see the solicitor, Mr. Waite, a two-story white frame house peaked in front of him at the top of the high ground. As he got closer to the dingy, neglected-looking building, butterflies fluttered around inside his stomach. *In one of those rooms in that clapboard and shingled house I'm going to talk to the man who signed those papers,* he thought as he got closer.

The plain front door of the building opened onto the first floor. On the second floor, Adam met Samuel Waite.

"Ahem," Adam said clearing his throat. "I'm not sure how to do this, sir." Adam held out his right hand. "I'm Adam Miller. My father was Henry Miller."

The man was on the portly side with a thick head of dark hair, and he wore a pair of spectacles low on his nose. He sat behind his desk, staring as though in shock while Adam stood offering his hand.

Suddenly, the man stood up, forcefully sending his chair against the wall behind him. His dark coat hung open. He took off his spectacles, taking a better look at the young man. "By God, you are," he said, rushing around the desk to take Adam's hand. As he touched it, he pulled Adam toward him and into his arms, and clutched the young man tightly.

"After all these years!" He now stood at arm's length in front of him. "You're safe and grown. So often I wondered if I'd done the right thing, sending you into the wilderness. I never heard from your aunt and uncle."

Adam reached inside to his upper coat pocket and pulled out his yellowed baptismal record and handed it to Samuel Waite. "This, I believe, you requested as my identification." While he spoke he reached down into his pants pocket and pulled out the gold watch. "And this," he added, unfastening the gold watch chain and laying the watch on Mr. Waite's desk.

The older man, in his early forties, still somewhat dazed, had a glazed look in his eyes as he reached for the items.

"Please sit down, my boy," he said. Excuse me if I seem a bit unraveled. The truth is I am."

He returned to the back of the desk, brought his chair to its place and sat down. Looking at the watch and the folded sheet of paper he said, "You see, I was doubtful of ever seeing these again." He carefully laid the watch down, and opened the paper. As though to further convince himself of the reality he put his spectacles on again and took time to read the information on the baptismal record.

"No doubt about it," he said. A smile covered his face. "You are Henry's son." He laid the paper on his desk and reached toward the center drawer in front of him. Opening it he lifted a small, framed pencil drawing from the drawer and looked at it carefully. "You look so much like him." His voice softened, almost fell away, "Except for your blond hair. That you got from your mother." Feeling a bit embarrassed at his rambling he handed the frame to Adam.

Not being able to remember what his father looked like, and having often wondered, Adam searched the penciled portrait for answers to so many questions. It was a formal drawing. His father stood, holding his gloves and top hat in his right hand; his left hand barely touched the left side of the hat. The painting gave the impression that he was a well-kept gentleman with dark hair and a trimmed mustache. Adam recognized the near smile on his face as that of his own. Looking at his hands and the stature of the man also brought a sense of recognition.

"He almost never looked like that," Mr. Waite said. "The painting was a gift, a practical joke, to me."

Adam looked up.

"You see," he said, "Henry, your father, hated to wear a dress coat. What he liked was to be out talking with people and working with them. He was in law practice, but he never looked like it, nor did he act like it." Now with a far away look in his eye, he said nothing. Adam watched him expectantly.

"Anyway, we were good friends, your father and me." A smile crossed his face. "I often gave him a talk on how a man of his social standing should dress and act.... It never did any good." The man chuckled. "To tell you the truth, I liked him the way he was."

Adam looked up from the painting and smiled. It was clear the man had loved his father. *I think I would have liked him too,* Adam thought still holding the drawing. As he handed it back to Mr. Waite he asked, "Did you know my mother well?"

"I did. Henry was lucky to have her. Freda was a lovely lady, not outstandingly beautiful but a real lady, with a sense of humor." He continued. "She had only one flaw that I know of..."

Adam was about to ask what it was, but Mr. Waite went on. "She loved your father too much. In the end that's what killed her." He paused and then explained. "After Henry's accident she lost her will to live."

Adam felt a flush come to his face as anger built inside of him. "She had me. I needed her love, too."

"So you did." The man took a moment to phrase his next words. "She missed him so much. She was lost without him, even when she looked at you, and she loved you dearly. You see, you looked so much like him, it broke her heart. Finally it got her down. It wore on her, til she was nothing but skin and bones. You were her son, but she desperately needed her husband, too."

"How could a mother do that to her own child?"

"Your mother didn't purposely do it, Adam. It just happened." The man looked at him with great tenderness. "I'm sorry."

Adam's anger ceased somewhat when he saw the understanding in Mr. Waite's eyes.

The two talked for a while longer until Mr. Waite said, "Adam, your parents left you some monies that I've invested for you."

Adam was about to ask more about this inheritance his Aunt had previously mentioned, but Mr. Waite continued.

"I've got to delve into this, get all the paperwork out and bring it up to date before I can give you the particulars." He looked up to the young man who now stood. "How long will you be here?"

"About a week I suppose. I came with some friends."

"Do you have somewhere to stay?"

Adam nodded.

"Can you come back tomorrow around noon? We can have lunch while we talk." He hesitated a moment. "Why didn't your Aunt write to me telling me you were safe?"

"At first they didn't know who I was," he explained. "They were afraid they'd lose me. Then when they knew who I was...," He looked at Mr. Waite and shrugged his shoulders. "Later, I guess, I don't know, but my Aunt did ask me to apologize for her. She told me she never knew what to write. She wanted to write and say thank you, but at the same time she missed her sister so badly."

Mr. Waite held out his hand to shake Adam's. "You are alive and well and I'm grateful for that." They shook each other's hand. "See you tomorrow."

As Adam walked down the crest of the hill he looked at the gold watch Mr. Waite had returned to him. They had talked for less than an hour. Already, he knew that the knowledge and feeling he'd gotten from the time he'd spent with Mr. Waite had changed him.

CHAPTER 10
A Sidecut

That evening, Adam found himself lost in his own thoughts.

Joe pulled him out of his reverie. "Adam, would you like to read this week's edition of *The Ohio Whig*?"

He looked at the newspaper the older man held out to him. "Yes, I would," he said, and reached to take it.

"There's an article in it about the bridge they're building across the river to Perrysburg."

"Where's it going to be?" Jake asked.

"Where the ferry goes across now. Once the bridge gets done there'll be two ways to cross the river."

"That'll be a long bridge!"

"Uh huh, it will," his uncle agreed.

Adam read the article on the front page about the bridge, then he opened the paper. Immediately his eye caught the headline, "Canal Irishman Accused of Robbery." He read it.

Another article discussed the straggling settlements of Irish workers between the canal towns. It went on to tell about the insufficient housing for the Irish laborers and their families. Adam continued to read and then scanned the last page. Finally he laid the paper down.

Jake and Joe were playing checkers again and nearing the end of a game. Adam waited until Joe, with a smile conquered the last of Jake's kings.

"Want to play another?" Joe asked his nephew.

"Sure, but this game has 'my name' on it!"

"Set it up," Joe said and looked over at Adam. "Something puzzling you?" he asked.

"I read those articles about the canal workers. Don't the people in Maumee like the canal workers?" Adam asked.

"Those Irish are a lot of rowdies, too fond of their whiskey and their fighting and who-knows-what else. They're an energetic lot, and the canal would never have gotten built without them. Still, their off-spring might not have any milk to drink, but you can be sure, there's much stronger drink around."

"Do the people of Maumee feel the same way about the Indians?"

"The Indians drink too much, but unlike the Irish, they don't have energetic ways about them."

"What do you mean?" asked Adam.

"They're a lazy people."

"Have they always been that way?"

"It's the ones that didn't move out with their tribe. There was not much for them to do once the reservations were closed."

"Why didn't they go with them?"

"They felt they belonged here, that they're part of the land. A few Indians married locals and couldn't leave; some are just rebels who refuse to conform."

"If you'd been an Indian, would you have gone with the Ottawa tribe when it was forced to those wild lands west of the Mississippi?"

Joe, a surprised look on his face answered, "I don't know; I never thought about it."

"I also read the article about the canal sidecut," Adam said as he got up from his chair and walked toward Joe. He handed the paper back to him.

"What sidecut?" Jake asked Adam, starting the new game of checkers.

"The article says the sidecut is to go from the canal into the Maumee River and then join in with the traffic in Lake Erie. I'd like to see that area." Adam looked at Jake. "Do you suppose we could use the buggy in the morning? It'd be interesting to see how they are going to start this sidecut. Do you think your mother would mind?"

"I'll ask her."

"Good." Adam looked once more at Joe and said. "The canal section they're building now, isn't it eventually supposed to hook up with the Miami Canal coming from Cincinnati to Piqua?"

"That's what I've read," Joe said to Adam. He leaned over and mussed Jake's hair. "When it's through," he said to him, "You and Tille will be able to come see us by canal boat."

The next morning Adam and Jake started out at daybreak to see the sidecut. The canal itself was to go another sixteen miles downstream until it reached Lake Erie. While driving toward the area of activity they could see two long rows of stakes, all driven into the ground, the rows forty feet apart. As they rode in the buggy they followed the sidecut stakes until they could see Irish beginning to clear the wooded areas between the rows. The smell of freshly sawed wood, whiffs of smoke, plus an aroma of burnt rye and bacon filled the air.

"Must be a worker's camp close by," Jake said. "Smells good to me."

They drove past the point of the felled trees. In the clearings, furrows were being cut by teams of oxen, pulling ploughs. The teams went across the clearing to the east, then to the west, and back again. A blade at the edge of each plough cut all roots up to two inches thick. The ploughman severed the thicker roots with his ax. Coming up behind them, pairs of oxen dragged scrapers going in the opposite direction, first going south, then to the north and back again. They scraped the loose dirt to the sides. Following close behind them, men with picks broke up more hard clay dirt. Others shoveled it into wheelbarrows and wheeled it up the sloping sides.

Adam and Jake watched the dirty and sweaty men exert themselves over the animals as the oxen expended their energies under the men's forcefulness. They were still overwhelmed at the sights they'd seen that morning when they returned the horse and buggy to the stable. However, during the interval the hands on the clock had moved to almost eleven o'clock. It was now time for Adam to meet Samuel Waite for lunch.

CHAPTER 11
An Inheritance

Samuel Waite was sitting at his desk leafing through pages of legal documents when Adam arrived. "How are you, son?" Mr. Waite asked when he saw him at his doorway. "Come in."

"I'm fine sir," Adam said as he entered the office.

"You hungry?"

"As a matter of fact I'm starved."

"Good, then let's head out to the tavern and get a bite." He pulled a sheet of paper from under the legal documents on his desk, folded it and put it in his inside jacket pocket.

They walked briskly in the late morning sunshine, Mr. Waite talking of Adam's father and some of the more memorable times they'd had together that he treasured. It was in great comfort that Adam sat beside his father's old friend and ate his way through his lunch. It made him feel like he belonged. As he finished his meal and was settling back on his chair, Mr. Waite pulled out the sheet of paper he'd put inside his jacket.

"I've a list here of the properties your money is invested in."

"Properties! There's more than one?"

"Four in all."

"What kind of properties?"

"There's your parents' home which is rented out, and a building in the business district. Another piece is out by the area of the new bridge, and there's some Black Swamp acreage."

"That much? What's it all worth?" Adam asked almost breathlessly. He now sat on the edge of his chair and looked questioningly at Mr. Waite.

"I haven't figured that out yet. It'll take a few days."

"I had no idea!" Adam said, almost to himself.

"I did my best by you, Adam."

"I appreciate that. That's not what I meant," he said apologetically, then looked at Mr. Waite squarely. "You see, I never dreamt there'd be monies and properties, and so much of it." He ran his hand through his blond hair.

"Your father was a very wise man," said Mr. Waite. "He wanted you and your mother taken care of. With your mother gone, too, it all comes to you." The serious look on Mr. Waite's face told Adam not to doubt his words. "You couldn't know and I fault myself for that. I should have tried to reach your aunt, but I was so lost without your father. It was a relief just to do the best I could for you with his money. Then later when I realized what a mistake I'd made by not making sure you were safe, I thought it was too late."

"But, you held on to the properties."

"I couldn't face the thought you might never come back. I couldn't have slept at night if I thought I'd sent you to your death."

Adam told him of how lucky he'd been to escape the wolves.

They talked on the way back to Mr. Waite's office. "It was such a relief to see you yesterday," Mr. Waite said. He opened his office door. "I have something else for you." He walked behind his desk and moved his chair out of the way. Then picked up a wooden chest and set it up on his desk. It covered more than half of his desktop. From the middle desk drawer he withdrew a key and placed it on the desk.

"What's this?" Adam asked, motioning toward the chest.

"I sorted through your parent's belongings after the funeral of your mother. Most of it went to the poor, but I kept a few items I thought you'd want. There could have been more, but I kept what I thought best." He stopped for a moment, his voice filled with emotion. "I'm sorry. This is all I have for you, of them." Tears rimmed his eyes. "Please forgive me."

Adam looked at him, his heart overwhelmed. "There is nothing to forgive. I thank you."

Mr. Waite went to him and put his arms around Adam. "You're so much like the two of them. I hope we can be friends."

"I do, too," Adam said.

"I have some business downstairs so I'll leave you to go through this by yourself." He blew his nose as he left.

Adam, numb with astonishment from what Mr. Waite had told him of the properties and of what set before him, slowly picked up the key, then laid it down again, not sure he was ready. Perhaps a whole minute went by while he wrestled with his emotions. Finally he again picked it up and this time unlocked the chest made of oak.

A quilt that covered a frame nearly pushed itself at Adam when he opened the lid. Carefully he pulled at the quilt-wrapped frame and then lifted the two out of the chest. A note pinned to the fold of the quilt read: *This quilt was made by Freda Miller. The chest was made by Henry Miller for his bride.*

Laying the quilt on the desk Adam carefully unfolded it until he saw the gold-leaf framed painting of his mother and father. A note attached read: *Wedding day of Freda and Henry Miller.* He recognized the similarities in looks of his mother and his aunt Trudy. After a time he let the painting lay face up on the desk and looked once more inside the chest. On one side of the chest, another smaller gold frame lay upside down. It was a pencil sketch of his mother and father holding a child of about two. *That must be me.* He placed it on top of the desk.

Nearly at the bottom of the chest lay a folder made of heavy fabric stretched over very thin board. He picked it up and opened it. A pencil sketch of a baby was inside. A note on the back said: *Adam Miller, age 3 months.* There was a certificate given to his father at the end of his legal schooling. Adam closed the folder and laid it beside the pictures on the desk.

Next he lifted out a family Bible. In it was the date of his birth and his parents' wedding date, his Aunt Trudy and Uncle Joseph's wedding date, and much more. He laid it down on the desk and looked again into the almost-empty chest. It still contained a velvet pouch and a small wooden box in a corner. Adam took them out and laid down the pouch. He took off the lid of the box. An empty ink bottle with a quill pen was inside. A note in fine handwriting was under the bottle and quill. Adam pulled it out and read:

To my darling Henry,
This is for you my dear, to use when you sign those
legal documents. I know there will be many.
Love,
Your Freda

A tear glistened at the edge of Adam's eye. He brushed it aside, and set the tiny box down. He picked up the black velvet pouch and loosened the string. Inside he found a cameo locket on a gold chain, and a gold wedding band. With them was a carefully folded note that read:

These belonged to Freda Miller.

On a piece of paper that was formed to fit inside the locket were the words:

My loves,
Henry and Adam.

Adam at that moment could feel the love of his parents he'd barely known. Any doubt he might have had about their not caring was gone. He pulled the gold pocket watch and chain from his pocket, loosened the clasp of the chain and slipped the gold wedding band on the watch chain. He put them back in his pocket. Carefully he put the cameo and chain back into the pouch and pulled the string tight. Then he returned all of the items to the chest.

As he finished, Mr. Waite came back into the office. Adam looked across the room and said, "You have given me a life I could only have hoped for."

"It is the least I could do." He walked behind his desk and put his hand on the chest. "Would you like to take this with you or leave it here until you're ready for your trip home?"

"I'll leave it here for now," Adam said.

"Let's take a walk then, and I'll show you a few of your properties. We won't be able to go inside your family home but you'll be able to see it." He picked up his hat. "We can go through the building in the business district. You might decide what you'd like to do with it. The man now occupying it would like to buy it. He'd offer you a fair price." Mr. Waite closed his office door. "Of course, it's your option, and with all this coming on you so quickly I don't want you to feel pressured."

The two left the house and went down the steps with Mr. Waite still talking. "The property down by the river is actually two parcels that are side by side. Your father loved to watch the river waters flow, so when those parcels became available I decided that purchasing them for you was probably what he would have wanted. They are bare ground but in a perfect location for whatever you think best."

The afternoon passed by swiftly. It was time for Adam to get back to Jake's family. He walked slowly, lost in the thoughts of what he'd discovered, heard, and seen in one short afternoon. *What should I do? If I sell the building in the business district what would I do with the money?* His mind reeled. So many questions for which he had no answers. Too soon he reached the house with the cobbler shop in front.

Joe was putting a "closed" sign in the window as Adam opened the door.

"Getting back at it?" Adam asked.

"Just a little. I had a customer in the short two hours I was open."

"You must have a thriving business," Adam said, and without thinking he asked Joe what he would do if he owned a building in the business district and someone wanted to buy it for a fair price. Would he sell it?

"Do you own one?"

"Yes," Adam answered almost hesitantly, as the feeling of ownership was so new to him.

"Do you need the money?"

"I don't have much of anything," he said, and thought *I'm not even sure what I want to do with my life. I never thought I had a choice until a few weeks ago.* Then he said to Joe. "It would make life a little easier for me, but no, I don't need it."

"So you could use it?"

"Yes. I could."

"Then I'd sell it. Put the money in a safe place until you need it. That's what I'd do."

"Thanks for your advice," Adam said appreciatively.

Joe, using his cane, started to go to the kitchen door. Adam followed.

The evening went slowly for Adam. He wanted some time alone to think, but there was little of it until he lay in bed beside Everett. And then, he fell asleep almost immediately.

CHAPTER 12
Decisions

Before daylight Adam awoke and lay quietly, running everything through his mind. By daybreak he had decided he'd sell the business building and put the money in a safe place until he needed it. He felt comfortable with that. And he'd ask Mr. Waite to continue to manage the two parcels and the home place properties for him. As for the Black Swamp acreage, he didn't quite understand why, but he wanted to look into that and take care of it himself.

He smelled bacon frying and the unpleasant aroma of burnt rye, instead of the more expensive aroma of coffee, before he was even out of bed. *It's been very pleasant being with Jake's family,* he thought as he pulled on his pants.

After breakfast he again went to see Mr. Waite. The two discussed Adam's decisions and agreed that Mr. Waite would manage the properties and would, this very afternoon, make arrangements for a quick sale of the business property. Also at Adam's request he agreed to get deeds of the other properties for Adam to see, and to keep, if he chose to take them with him.

"Why did you decide to buy the property in the Black Swamp area?" Adam asked.

"Your father was anxious to see the Ohio country opened. People in the wilderness areas had difficult lives. Henry felt that if the state would be opened it would make life easier for them, and the rest of the country would benefit as well." He sat down at his desk.

"When the state land agent began to sell tracts of land close to where the proposed canal was to go through I felt your father would have invested in that area. I looked at the names of the areas. I wasn't familiar with any of them." He looked at Adam and raised his hands. "After worrying about it awhile I decided to just go ahead and purchase some of the land, hoping I was doing right." Mr. Waite looked helplessly at Adam.

"I realize now, a little late, that the land is in a swampy area. However, the proposed canal is still going through there."

"You think it still has value then?" Adam asked.

"It probably isn't worth much now, but then the cost was relatively low, so by the time the canal is dug, a profit might easily be realized."

"I hope so. I think I'd like to check out that area myself." Adam told him. "I will keep in touch by letter, if you'd like that."

"I would," agreed Mr. Waite.

Walking back, he thought, *Mr. Charles had also purchased land in the swamp area unaware of the terrain. I wonder how many other people have done the same? I must check this swamp out.*
Once more he entered the cobbler shop where Joe was waiting on a young woman needing a pair of shoes repaired.

Three days later the trio was ready to make its way back to Schinbone in the wilderness. The weather had started to change as clouds had begun to gather.

"It looks like rain," said Joe, standing with his family, watching as they got into the buggy.

"Maybe it'll snow. It feels cold enough," said Tille.

"Have a safe trip," her sister-in-law, Edna said. The small group waved goodbye to each other as the buggy headed down the pathway.

Adam settled in the buggy as best he could, his gun within easy reach, his newly acquired chest, roped to the back of the buggy. He was as comfortable as possible.

While they rode he wondered, *How will Aunt Trudy react to all the things I have to tell her and to the things I'll show her?*

CHAPTER 13
Winter

The rains came after they arrived home. The mud came, too. Boots were sucked up inside the mire as Adam and his family went from shed to outhouse, back to the house. Mud clung to everything. Walking in it took extreme effort.

In a few weeks the weather turned cold. The mud froze so solid it could be walked on. Going to the shed, to the outhouse, and back to the house was easy walking, but terribly cold. When the wind blew and snow was flying, fine snow came through the cracks, between the outside logs and the inside slats of the house.

The fireplace, the hearth of the home, was the only place to stay warm when awake, and the morning started early. The feather bed was the only place to be warm at night.

The painting of Adam's parents hung above the fireplace mantle. When Adam first showed it to his aunt, she cried. So touched was he that he asked her, "Would you like to hang it where you can always see it?"

Without hesitation she took it from him and went to the fireplace. "Could we hang it here?" she asked. Joseph readily agreed and hung it promptly.

Almost every day Joseph and Adam covered the area where they set traps. They carried their guns for protection from wolves and to hunt small game, which was plentiful. Often during their outings they also picked up hickory nuts and walnuts.

The tall cottonwood trees dwarfed the men, along with the less tall trees of oak, elm, maple and ash, which they called by name. So familiar with the varieties were the families that even the settlers' children were able to recognize their names, and their differences in bark, in leaves and in nuts.

One day Adam and Joseph came across a stranger. His facial features suggested that he was of Indian blood. He stood to the side of one of the maple trees that the two passed by daily. Cautiously Adam and Joseph watched. Then, realizing that the Indian was pulling tobacco leaves from holes that had been previously chipped out of the trunk of the tree, the two walked up to the Indian.

Adam watched in interest. "Why do you pack it in those holes?" he asked.

"Makes good chew," the tall Indian said and offered a small handful of leaves to the two.

"Don't mind if I do," Joseph said taking the offering. Carefully he wadded up a small amount as the Indian had done. "The plug tastes of the maple sap," Joseph said. Why don't you try it?" He said to Adam.

Like Joseph, he'd not had this kind of chew before. He put a very small portion in his mouth. For a moment he chewed as the Indian and Joseph watched. Suddenly he spit the wad from his mouth and spat several more times trying to rid himself of the tobacco taste.

"I don't think it tasted of maple sap." Adam said as he and his uncle walked on their way.

"The flavor was bitterer than I expected, too."

"It was a new experience," Adam said.

That evening Adam thought about all the new experiences he'd had that fall. He remembered Mr. Charles, too, and wondered what new experiences he'd have, because of their friendship. It gave him food for thought.

CHAPTER 14
June 1839
The Swamp

All winter long he'd thought and wondered what this swamp might look like. Now it was mid-June, and he was in the midst of it. *I probably should be home helping with the farming,* he thought as he trudged through the mud puddles and deep water, swatting at mosquitoes. *There's not a bird to be seen, nor heard,* he thought. Sweat dripped from his pores, and the pesky insects swarmed around his face, landing and sucking his blood from any place they could sit before Adam smashed them with his large hands.

The air felt heavy and smelled of rotting wood and decaying vegetation. *This muck they want to clear for a canal?* He questioned their wisdom as a brownish-black water moccasin slithered through the jungle of growth that was everywhere. *This is what Mr. Charles and Mr. Waite purchased as investment land?*

Disgustedly he turned around from his short trek inland and went back to where he'd tethered his horse. *The canal will never get dug through here,* was all he could think as he reached for the horse's reins. *This poor horse, even out here at the edge of this swamp, has been bitten unmercifully.* "Let's get out of here," he said to his horse as he nudged him with his heels.

After riding two miles through the woods he saw the small clearing ahead. Just knowing it was there, with the swamp behind him, brought welcome relief. Once back in the clearing he stopped the horse and set foot on solid ground. From the saddle horn he loosened the leather bag that held his drinking water. *What were those engineers thinking when they mapped out this route for the canal? More than likely, they've never set eyes on the place,* he thought as he walked his horse. His mind still reeled from the shock of the dismal swamp.

Yet, as he headed back toward Schinbone along the canal route, he eventually came upon new sections of canal being dug and more land being cleared going in the direction from where he'd just been.

That evening, his heart heavy, he stopped for the night at one of the many taverns along the route. He pushed open the heavy plank door, to a loud and harsh conversation about Ohio's financial instability.

"We haven't received any wages for months," one red-faced worker with heavy jowls said, complaining loudly as his mug of ale foamed over onto the dirt floor.

"Well, that's better than us," said another. "We got paid in the state's borrowed, Michigan 'wildcat' money, which turns out not to be worth the paper it's printed on."

"Oh yeah, how's that worse?" The first man quarreled, grabbing the second man's shirt collar with his free hand.

Not wishing to be in the center of the threatened brawl Adam skirted the area around them and found an empty table in a corner. A couple sat nearby talking quietly, trying to ignore the bedlam. When the barmaid made it to Adam's seat he ordered a mug of ale. "And is there an empty bunk available to sleep in tonight?" he asked before she hurried away.

"You get the last one, sir, unless you want the end room we have left."

"The bunk will be fine."

As she left to get his order and make sure he got the bunk, a young woman entered with a well-dressed gentleman. Her long dress and dark hair reminded him of Alese. Quite unexpectedly he felt an emptiness in his stomach.

"Your bunk is ready anytime," the barmaid told him when she brought his mug.

He ordered a bowl of warm, thick chicken soup, boiled potatoes, and bread, which was served on a gray and white speckled granite plate and bowl. Finishing, he headed for his bed.

The sleeping room contained four narrow bunks. Three men a few years older than Adam lay on their backs, all waiting for sleep to come and the air to become cooler as it came through the one open window, covered with thin white gauze to keep out the insects.

He took off his boots and lay down on the empty bunk, tiredness engulfing him. He was certain he'd fall asleep quickly.

"Have you seen the acreage they want to flood for that reservoir?" one of the men in the dark room asked of another.

"I was there a few weeks ago. It's hard to believe they'll get all the trees down and everything cleaned out before they dam up the streams!"

Adam listened intently. "Where's this place you're talking about?" he asked.

"Down by Fort St. Marys," the first man said. "Have you been there?"

"I've been to Fort St. Marys; seen the canal area, but not a reservoir."

"It's west of the canal. A feeder leads right to it."

"Two feeders," the second man said. "One on the east end and one on the south end."

"It's a sight for sure," said the first man. "You gotta see it."

"I'm heading that way in the morning," Adam said.

"Will you guys shut up," the third man said. "I'd like to get some sleep tonight."

The conversation died quickly, but Adam's mind was still going. *I'll never get to sleep now, no matter how tired I am.* However, after a half-hour, in which he tried to envision the reservoir, he fell into a deep slumber.

Later, Adam's sleep turned uneasy. When daylight finally chased the darkness away he did not feel rested. Habit though, and an urgent desire to see this huge reservoir at Fort St. Marys helped to waken him and got him started on his way.

For the better part of the day he rode his horse, still following the canal route towards his destination, and passing more sections of the canal being dug. At these, he took time to rest his horse while he studied the ways in which the different crews were going about making this big ditch.

Some were professional in their manner of organization and procedures. Others went about their job haphazardly. At one section he talked with the contractor who had bid to get his section of the project. A laborer, at another section, told him his project was being spearheaded by a farmer who owned the property that the canal passed through.

By the time Adam neared Fort St. Marys, he'd learned quite a bit about digging and building canal banks, getting rid of tree stumps, putting clay on the bottom of the canal to keep the water in, how locks were made, what type of soil was in different sections, which direction the water would flow, and why. Stopping as often as he had put him behind in travel time.

Two hours before darkness descended, he realized he was of equal distance to Fort St. Marys as he was to Schinbone. He could reach either while it was still daylight.

In the morning I can get a clear view of that reservoir, he thought as he chose to follow the canal and stay in Fort St. Marys.

Once again, deciding to pay to use a sleeping room, he was glad he'd brought home some of the monies from the sale of the building in Maumee. He was also glad he'd kept the rest of it safe for use at another time.

When he'd purchased his horse, guilt had touched him. He hadn't needed the horse, but having it made it so much easier for him to get around. Now guilt was niggling at him again.

After all, my parents left the money for me to use. I'm not wasting it! Fleetingly he wondered what life might be like if he did. Then shook his head.

CHAPTER 15
The Big Dig

By early the next morning he was on his horse. The reservoir lay three miles west of the St. Marys section of the canal. Anxious as he was, it still took him a short time to ride those miles. He came upon the north end of the reservoir area almost without knowing it.

A natural elevation existed on the northern and southern shorelines of the proposed man-made lake. Adam was on the northern end.

One of the men, last night, had said the distance across, from one side to the other was four miles. *I believe he was right,* he thought as he measured the distance by eye. He also measured by eye the varied distances of the embankments. One was two miles long, the other four. The height seemed to vary from ten to twenty-five feet.

Adam followed a path to the feeder on the east end. After a while he came to the southeastern elevation. A rider came up from the woods to stand beside him. Shortly the man said, "In Columbus at the state office, they call this the 'big dig.'"

The tall thin man looked vaguely familiar. Both looked at the activity going on below them. The man got off his horse. Adam dismounted in like fashion. Together they walked slowly westward. At the bottom, were men, dump-carts, horses, and, teams of oxen.

The men were felling trees on the inside edges of the reservoir in front of the black willows which bordered the heavy marsh grass. Teams of oxen were pulling whole trees over to piles of trees that had been left to dry. Large areas, purposely burned of their under grown hay, now blackened with ash and smoke, lay toward the far-western end of the reservoir.

Adam continued to look but was bothered by the gentleman. *I wish I could remember who this man is.*

"You interested in the canal for a reason?" the man asked.

"I'd like to see it go through. It'd be the best thing for the farmers," Adam said as he walked on a bit. "I'm not so sure it'll happen though."

"Why is that?"

"I own some land further up north in the worst of the swamp where the canal's going to be dug. I've just come from there. I don't see how anything can get past that depressing, wild and wet place. And, it stinks to high heaven!"

"Some of the men that are doing the digging have dug before, in places almost as bad."

"How do you know?"

"I'm a state canal commissioner."

"Your face looks familiar, but I don't know that we've met."

"We've not. You saw us in the tavern, night before last. A woman friend and I were having a discussion when you sat down in the corner near us."

"Now I remember," Adam said and introduced himself.

"Even if they could dig it," Adam said, "the area's so full of mosquitoes the men would be bitten to death."

"We've got something for that."

"What?" Adam wanted to know.

"Coal oil. Mosquitoes can't stand the smell or taste."

Adam doubted that last statement after smelling the swamp, himself, but he said nothing. "Who owns the land around here?" he asked.

"The Federal government gave most of the land to the state. The local owners have sold out and are moving elsewhere."

Near the black willows Adam could see log cabins and outbuildings standing empty. Fences were squared off around them.

The two continued looking down into the 'big dig.' "It will cover twenty-seven square miles," said the commissioner. "At the western end of the reservoir lies Beaver Creek and the new village called Celina. It was platted out only five years ago." He turned, pointing toward the southern-most tip. "Montezuma's there. This reservoir will hold enough water to keep the canal's water level the same for sixty miles."

"Do you think they'll get the reservoir bottom cleared and the farmers paid for their crops before they let in the water?"

"That was the deal." The two walked for a while longer. "There's nearly 18,000 acres here."

"Man alive!" Adam said in amazement looking at the area the dig covered. "How many men are working on it?"

"On the western embankment where the big pit is, there are about 500," the commissioner answered. "It's my job to make sure they do their jobs."

He looked directly at Adam and, held out his right hand. "I'm glad to have met you," he said. "I've been in front of you and behind you in your travels these past few days. I hope what you've learned will be of advantage to you. You seem to have a level head on your shoulders."

Adam shook the man's hand and once again mounted his horse. Turning it around, he headed back toward the eastern feeder path. As he followed it, he saw the shanties where the canal workers lived. *Nothing but boards nailed together and planks on top for a roof,* he thought. *These men earn their wages. I'd need a jigger or two of whiskey myself if I worked as hard and had to live in those shacks.*

At the end of the feeder was the canal. A bit south of it was Lock Eleven. The town of St. Marys was a mile north. It had taken him the better part of the morning and a good part of the afternoon to see everything. He was tired, yet he was filled with excitement. *Feels like I have bubbles in my blood,* he thought, as he headed southeast, toward Schinbone and Freedom.

"We're going home," he said as he gently slapped the long neck of his horse.

It was nearly dusk, and the trees cast dark shadows on the narrow wagon trail as Adam rode nearer to Freedom. *Home will be a welcome sight*, he thought.

As he came within earshot he heard dogs barking and his name being called.

"Adam, Adam, help me!" The voice came from the shed. Quickly he turned the horse toward it and jumped to the ground. "Help me." Marcus called again.

Adam ran through the open doorway to find his cousin in a half-sitting position leaning against the feedbox. His right leg from the knee on down stuck out strangely away from his body. "What happened?" Adam asked.

Tears welling in Marcus' eyes, "I fell from the beam," he said. "I was trying to cross it with my hands and I lost my grip."

"How long have you been out here like this?"

"I just fell. I tried to get up right before I heard your horse."

"Hold on a minute, I'll go get your pa. Looks like your leg's broken."

Adam patted his horse on the rump as he went past him going toward the house. "I'll be right back to unsaddle you."

Joseph came out of the cabin when Adam was nearly there. "Heard the dogs and then saw the horse. Glad you're back."

"Marcus is hurt. He fell, was hanging from the center beam. Trying to hand walk it. He broke his leg, I think.

"Go get Trudy," Joseph said. "I'll see to Marcus 'til she gets out here."

CHAPTER 16
An Agreement

For a week Adam helped Joseph on the farm. Marcus' broken leg made him unable to do much, so Adam offered to do more work for a while.

It was during that week that Joseph and Adam made plans to add to the shed and make it into a real barn. Whenever they discussed it Joseph's eyes lit up.

"I'll buy the nails when I take my horse into town," said Adam.

"Don't you think it's time to give your horse a name?" Joseph asked.

"I've been thinking of naming him. He's such a good animal to have and such a relief. So far I haven't come up with a name."

"Call him Relief," said Marcus, who was now ten, having just had a birthday. His eyes were bright with the prospect of possibly having given the horse a name.

"Not much of a name for a horse. Yet, I don't know...it sort of fits him," Joseph told the two.

"I'll give it some thought," Adam said.

Joseph returned to the subject of the barn, "We've enough logs cut from last fall, and we've a beam or two."

"Can we get a few pigs?" Marcus wanted to know.

"I think so," his pa said.

Adam could remember when he first came to his aunt and uncle's and how excited he'd been to see the lean-to on the side of the house. He remembered their cow and horse in the shed. Everything had seemed so large to him then.

Now there was Marcus, who just turned ten, Seth, eight, and little Freda, now five. The family had grown. It was time for the shed to grow, too.

"I'll buy some extra hardware and a few bolts," said Adam.

"As good as done," said Joseph. "Now, when do you think you'll want to get started?" he asked Adam.

"I've been planning to go back to Piqua, to see Mr. Charles, in a few days. We're almost caught up here. Can you take care of everything for about a week?" He looked towards Joseph who nodded his head.

"Seth's been wanting to help out some. It's time he learns how."

"Good. Then let's plan on starting when I get back, and all the work is caught up."

"We'll do it," said Joseph.

It was Tuesday. Four days later Adam started on his way to Piqua. Leaving early in the morning he made it to Sidney before dark. Again he paid to use a sleeping room above the tavern.

At daybreak, he was on his horse, and by noon riding into Mr. Charles' pathway. Automatically he looked toward the second story window. He saw no sign of anyone. Nudging his horse, he slowly circled around to the back of the house. *Wonder if Andrew's around; I kind of miss him,* he thought. *It would be nice to see Alese, too. More than just nice,* he thought. He felt his heart skip a beat, and a flush come to his face. He pulled back on the reins, hoping to give himself time to let the flush disappear.

It was Mr. Charles that he saw first, slowly ambling around the corner of the barn. Shoulders erect but head down, almost like his life energy had been drained. Andrew followed a good ten feet behind, walking as though he'd lost his best friend. He neither saw nor heard Adam until he cleared his throat.

Both down faces looked his way. Momentarily they stood staring.

"Adam," Andrew said and broke into a run toward him.

"Is that really you?" Mr. Charles asked, his face brightening. His walk perked up as he, too, headed toward Adam who still sat in his saddle.

What has happened? Adam wondered as he got down from his horse. Andrew ran forcefully into him as Adam's feet hit the ground, nearly shoving him against his horse. His arms wrapped around Adam's waist, the boy broke into sobs.

Adam put his own arms around the boy's shoulder's holding him close. Slowly he moved his hand, and held him out to see his face. What could be so wrong that Andrew would attach himself to him so emotionally? They didn't know each other well enough to be that close. "What's wrong, Andrew?" he asked as Mr. Charles walked up, perceptibly in a brighter mood, but noticeably low in spirit.

"Pa died." Andrew sobbed, trying to control his crying.

"We buried him day before yesterday," Mr. Charles said.

Adam, full of questions spurted out. "How? Where?"

"He was having a spell," Andrew said, barely able to hold his voice steady.

Adam walked to the barn fence and tied his horse as they talked.

"Dr. O'Ferral said it must have been his heart," Mr. Charles said, looking with sympathy at the boy. The three walked for a bit until they had talked through the details of the last few days.

"And how's your Ma doing?" Adam asked Andrew, who now had his emotions under control.

"She sits in their room most of the time," he answered almost in a whisper.

"Who's been taking care of the house and the cooking?"

"Alese some," Mr. Charles said. "Mostly we're just getting by." At the mention of Alese's name Adam felt an extra beat in his chest.

"Let's go inside," said Mr. Charles, "and see if we can put together something to eat."

Andrew looked up at the two men, "I'll go tell Ma you're here. She'll be pleased." He went off in another direction as Mr. Charles and Adam moved towards the kitchen.

"Where's Alese?" Adam asked.

"She went into town this morning. There were some legal things that needed to be taken care of. Margaret just isn't able to do it right now, so Alese is doing as much as she can for her. It's difficult for her, though. She took her father's death hard, too."

As they got closer to the kitchen they heard loud banging noises. Pushing open the door, they saw Mrs. Elizabeth banging around pots and pans. "I'm trying to find a skillet. It's been so long since I've done any cooking," she said with a look of helplessness on her face.

"I'll do it," said Adam. "Put the fixings out here," he said, taking charge.

Just then Andrew's Ma came hurrying through the doorway. "Oh, no you don't. Not in my kitchen. It's my duty to do the cooking; now all of you just go!" Standing in front of Adam, she smiled. "I see we have one more for lunch. Good to see you again," She bent over to pull a skillet from a bottom cupboard.

Adam walked to Margaret and took her hand. "I'm so sorry about your husband. If I can help you in any way, please let me know."

"Thank you, I know you would," Margaret said. For a moment she was lost for words. Recovering quickly she said, "I've got to get busy. You're hungry, aren't you?"

"Yes, ma'am."

"Then scoot for now."

Mr. Charles, a smile beginning to curve his lips upward said, "Let's you and me go to the study. A little life was again starting in his eyes.

"Don't either of you go too far away," said Mrs. Elizabeth. "The two of us are fixin' something quick, aren't we, Margaret?"

Andrew's mother looked at Mrs. Elizabeth in disbelief. Then quickly agreed. "You heard her; it'll be ready soon."

Within the hour they ate lunch. Afterwards, Adam and Mr. Charles again found their way to the study.

"I've been to the area of your swamp property. The same route that the canal will take," said Adam.

"What did you think?"

"I was..." he stopped. Then started again. "It's awful there. It stinks terrible, it's murky, the woods are so thick, and, swamp water is everywhere. Snakes crawl around, and mosquitoes near ate me alive."

"That bad, huh?" Mr. Charles said aloud, a look of disappointment shadowing his face. "Did I make a mistake then, buying that land?"

"I thought so when I first came away from it, but as I headed back toward home I saw many new sections of the canal being dug. At St. Marys I rode out to see the reservoir." Adam related his impressions of what he'd seen. "I met one of the state canal commissioners there."

"What did he have to say about the swamp area?"

"I told him what I'd seen and what I thought," said Adam. "He was calm enough, didn't seem worried. As we watched men down in the reservoir working, he told me not to concern myself, and said the canal men had dug in places nearly as bad. He says they can do it."

Mr. Charles sat down in one of the leather-covered chairs and motioned to Adam to have a seat, too. "After seeing all of that, what do you think?"

"The commissioner's probably right, but I wouldn't want to be one of the men doing the digging. Those men live in shacks and work as hard as their animals. I couldn't do it."

"What could you do, Adam?" Mr. Charles asked, rearranging himself in the chair.

"I don't know."

"Are you still interested in getting the Ohio territory opened?"

"Yes, sir, I am," he said adamantly.

"If you're not interested in digging the canal then, would you be interested in traveling on it?"

"What do you mean?" Adam asked, a curious look on his face.

"I'm not sure yet," Mr. Charles said contemplating. "Maybe on one of the canal boats?"

"As a hired hand?"

"It's been rumored that one of the canal boat captains is going to have to sell his boat. He's in failing health. Would you consider that?"

"Buying a boat? Being a captain?" Adam asked incredulously.

"I think you have what it takes, and you've traveled most of the canal route north."

Adam interrupted, "I was up to Maumee a short time ago, and watched a sidecut being dug." Realizing then that he'd spoken out of turn, he quieted.

"As I said," Mr. Charles went on, "You've seen a good deal of the canal route. Do you think you'd like to travel on it and earn your living that way?"

Adam sat back on his chair and let air blow out through his lips.... "Whew, I never figured on anything like that...but yes, I think I could do it."

Mr. Charles continued, "I'd buy the boat; you'd do the traveling and make the boat pay. Would you consider it?"

"I don't know much about doing business on the canal."

"You're a competent and resourceful young man. I'm sure you can handle it." Mr. Charles looked directly at Adam. "Can I take it then that you're open to this arrangement? I purchase the boat, you take command of it, operate the day to day business of it, and we share equally in the profits?" Mr. Charles moved to the edge of his chair as he talked.

"How soon would all this come about, and how would I learn the business?" Adam asked, his voice a bit shaky. "I promised my uncle that I'd help him build a barn when I get home."

"I have a friend who owns his own boat and is his own captain. Let me talk with him about taking you under his wing for the rest of the season, after you get the barn built. Would that be agreeable with you?"

Adam slowly nodded his head. "Yes, but you hardly know me. You're taking a big risk!"

"I prefer to think of you as an investment, and with every investment there's a gamble. I'll worry about my vulnerability if you'll keep your end of the deal." He looked at Adam as he got up from his chair. Holding out his hand he said, "A gentlemen's agreement then, for now. By the season's end, I'll have it on paper."

Adam reached to shake the hand as his head spun. *It was a perfect chance for me to learn a new business without risking my own money.* He nodded.

"Partners we are then," Mr. Charles said, a happy smile covering his face.

An Aqueduct

PART THREE

CHAPTER 1
August 1839
Captain Elias Conners

Adam, square shouldered, wavy blond hair cut to mid-ear and to the neckline in the back, his face clean-shaven, the scar on the bottom of his chin barely noticeable, stood tall, in sharp contrast to Captain Elias Conners.

The shorter captain, narrow in width, wore his straight, coal-black hair as long as his ear lobes. Long dark eyelashes and heavy bushy eyebrows topped his deep, gray-blue eyes. His wide full mustache blended into a heavy beard that hung below the points of his shirt collar, and was as black as his full head of hair.

"They make a pair!" people said with a chuckle when they saw them together, which was quite often.

Elias' canal boat was a cross between a freight boat and a packet, which was called a line boat. He steered his boat from Piqua to Dayton and then on to Cincinnati, and he preferred to haul freight. "Hauling people takes special handling," he told Adam. "My boat is too rough for fine ladies. If we haul passengers let's try to keep it to men."

On Adam's first day of working on the canal he walked every square inch of the twelve by sixty-four-foot long boat. It took him three minutes from front to back, which included dodging a few passengers and parts of the bulky freight. Afterwards he wondered, *Can I live in a space as small as this?*

Yet he found docking, and boating on the canal quite interesting. When they passed through a series of locks the first time, even though Adam was busy, with his eight-foot pole pushing at one of the side walls of the lock, helping to center the boat inside it, his attention was captured. So thrilled was he, that as the boat moved slowly up and down, whenever he had a free minute he looked around at the passengers to see if they, too, were amazed.

Often as the days went by, he watched small herds of deer graze at the edge of the passing forest. He knew that quickly the image might be replaced by several fox chasing a fawn. At other times he saw small fields of planted corn. *Nothing's for long,* he realized as the boat was pulled steadily forward by the slow-moving mules.

He chuckled out loud the first time he heard the cry "low bridge." The men passengers who were airing themselves on the top deck scooted and clambered down the side ladders, barely in time to prevent themselves from being pushed off into the murky water by the upcoming bridge.

Life was exciting, yet peaceful as he absorbed the ways of canal boating. However, learning the business of trading, as a way of making a living, was a different story.

Generally, forwarding agents handled freight fees for consignment goods for the canal boats, but not always.

Adam was a farmer at heart, and farmers were his friends. He talked with them and identified with them. When they discussed fees with Adam they went away wearing smiles. Not only because they enjoyed their conversations, but also because they left secure in the knowledge that they had been treated fairly. There were times, though, while dealing with Adam, that he charged the farmers less than Elias could afford.

"Forget you are a farmer, and remember that you no longer make your living toiling in the fields, or raising livestock, but from this canal boat business," said Elias, his tone harsh.

Embarrassed, but with his heart still with the farmers, Adam defended his actions. "They can't afford high freight costs. They need all the money they can get. They've worked hard."

"Certainly they have, but we can't haul for them if we can't make any money." Tersely, Captain Elias added, "We need to eat, too!"

Later Elias sat down with him. They went over the books together.

"It's hard to remember I'm not a farmer," Adam said. The answering frown from Captain Elias encouraged Adam to quickly add, "But I'll remember from now on."

Still in his trading, however well intentioned, his heart went out to the farmer. The fourth time it happened, Elias, wearing a stern look on his face, said, "I think it best I take care of the trading we have to do." He quickly relieved Adam of that part of canaling. The next day the boat docked in Hamilton to take on a male passenger who was riding only a short distance, and paying three cents a mile.

As Adam took the man's money he looked up to see a young man of color walking along the tow path, and realized he knew him.

Hurriedly he put the passenger's money in his pocket, welcomed him on board and yelled, "Hey Thomas."

The two met in front of the General Store. "Thomas," Adam greeted him. "What are you doing here?"

"Picking up my mother from my uncle's packet boat," Thomas answered. "She's been staying with my aunt. Uncle Ralph is bringing her home."

"Your uncle's the captain?"

"Yes," Thomas nodded.

"Have you ridden on the packet?" Adam asked.

"A few times." Hearing the interest in Adam's voice he asked, "Would you like to see the boat?"

"Sure would." Stopping, Adam looked back at Elias' boat for a moment. "Let me tell my captain where I'll be."

Shortly the two stood together, waiting and watching for Thomas' uncle's bright-blue colored packet boat.

After it docked several passengers got off. One man wanting to get on, to go to Cincinnati was charged four cents a mile, thirty-seven cents for dinner including a shot of whiskey, and an extra one-half cent for a bed, before he was let on. After he paid his fees Adam and Thomas boarded.

Unlike Elias' boat, the packet carried no heavy freight but transported the mail and up to thirty pounds of free luggage for each passenger. People slept as well as dined on the packet. Looking around the fourteen-foot wide by seventy-four foot long boat, Adam marveled at how the main cabin furnishings could be changed so quickly.

The dining area changes into a sleeping area, he remembered Thomas telling him the first time Adam saw the three-foot wide stretched canvas shelves which had been turned into beds the night before.

The area now contained one long table with chairs around it for passengers to use while eating and socializing.

Thomas, touching a chest-high counter containing shelves underneath, said, "This becomes a bar in the early evening." They were walking through the dining area toward the captain's quarters. "My mother should be waiting up there for me," he said pointing to the cabin ahead. They passed a small curtain-covered ladies-room and several passengers.

I wish I could talk with them, Adam thought. *It'd be interesting to hear where they've been.*

Thomas opened the door to his uncle's cabin. A woman in her late forties, a bonnet on her head and a carpetbag by her feet, sat on the edge of the captain's lower bunk. Her rather plain face developed a wide smile when she saw Thomas, who gave her a light kiss on the cheek. She stood to hug him.

"Mother," Thomas said, "this is Adam Miller. I met him on my trip back from Cincinnati. He works for Captain Conners."

Still smiling she said, "Isn't this a wonderful way to travel? We passed all kinds of boats. It was such great fun, and not a bump," she said. "Well, that's not true," she laughed a tinkling laugh. "When we went through the locks we did get several bumps, but it's been so exciting! The water bridge was just wonderful, too. Who'd have guessed a canal boat could go above a river and still be on the canal?"

"The water bridge is called an aqueduct, Mother," Thomas said.

"There was another kind of bridge that went over the water," she said. I think they called it a culvert?"

"That's right, Mother."

Adam smiled at her excitement. "Let me carry that," he said picking up the bag that sat on the bunk behind her. Continuing the conversation he asked, "How long did it take you to get here?"

"Twenty-four hours, just one day!" she said.

"When I rode with Captain Conners and Adam it took us over a day and a half didn't it?" Thomas asked Adam.

He nodded in agreement. "Hauling freight weighs down our boat. It moves slower, usually about two miles an hour."

As they went back through the boat, Adam looked wistfully at the long open windows. He was very aware that this boat had a roof as well as high sides, providing more protection from the weather. In the center of the boat was a stable for the mules. On the stable walls Adam saw cages of chickens, geese and rabbits. His mouth watered at the thought of the food selection that was available on the packet.

"I never rode on a packet boat," said Adam.

"You should take a ride on one," Thomas' mother said.

"You're welcome to come with us," said a man, who had just laid his arm on Thomas' shoulders. "We sometimes go top speed at four miles an hour, but not any faster. We don't want our waves to wash away the banks."

Turning toward the man Thomas said, "This is my Uncle Ralph."

"I would like to take a ride one day," Adam said as they stepped off the boat. Standing on the bank he looked back at the great number of people sunning themselves on the top deck of the boat. "How many passengers do you carry?"

"Today we have thirty-five but we can carry as many as forty."

"That makes it pretty crowded doesn't it?"

"Not if the weather's nice. Some passengers ride on the upper deck. Otherwise, it does get crowded for a few folks, but we get everyone where they want to go," the man said. He held out his hand. "It's nice to meet a friend of Thomas.'"

From behind, Adam heard Elias' voice. "Hello there, Ralph."

The captain turned, and with a smile shook hands with Elias. "Good to see you again." The two talked momentarily in front of the trio, and then Captain Ralph introduced Elias to them.

"I already know this young man," Elias said grinning. He looked toward Adam. "He's a friend of Charles."

"So you're the one he has taken such a liking to," Captain Ralph said, rubbing his stubble-free chin.

"I guess so," Adam said, his face reddening. *Mr. Charles must know everyone,* he thought.

"I saw him yesterday," Captain Ralph said to Elias. "He told me he was hoping to see you this week, on your return trip.

Elias looked pleased. "I'll look forward to that," he said. "He's a good friend."

And, you'll have to tell him how poorly I'm doing at trading! Thought Adam, already wondering what Mr. Charles was going to say. And that maybe he wasn't *meant* to be a captain of a canal boat after all. *Maybe I shouldn't have been so quick to take Mr. Charles up on his offer.*

Cargo Boat

CHAPTER 2
September 1839
The Freight Packet

"Adam, Elias, it's good to see you," said the portly Mr. Charles. He wore his usual suit, vest, and tie. His pocket watch chain hung neatly on the right side of his dark trousers.

I'm going to disappoint him. He's counting on me. Adam thought as he smiled to welcome his partner while butterflies fluttered about inside his stomach.

Mr. Charles' hand reached for Adam's.

Adam in turn clasped his friend's. His smile felt forced. *Maybe he'll understand.* Adam pumped the older man's hand.

Elias, smiling broadly, could barely contain his excitement at seeing Mr. Charles.

The three stood on the Piqua canal bank in front of a new Merchant Tailor's Store. Adam, about to comment on a remark of Elias', looked up to see young Andrew coming toward them.

As he had the last time he'd seen him, the boy ran toward him, again nearly knocking him down. Adam laughed in pure pleasure as the youngster, now eleven, lovingly wrapped his arms around him.

A feeling of warmth eased itself around Adam, clothing him in momentary contentment as he returned the boy's hug. "Have you been taking good care of my horse?" he asked Andrew when the two had separated.

"Every day, and I've been exercising him, too, like you asked." Andrew beamed. "He's getting used to me now."

"I knew I could count on you." He ruffled the boy's brown hair.

Andrew looked up. "Thanks," he said, reaching to smooth his hair with his hands.

Mr. Charles turned from Elias to look at Adam, still talking and enjoying being with Andrew. The two older men who had fallen back while conversing had separated, and Mr. Charles walked toward them, a glint of pride showing in his eyes.

Andrew stopped in mid-sentence when he saw Mr. Charles approaching.

"Andrew," Mr. Charles said, "could you get your mother's basket from the buggy?"

"Sure," he said. Quickly turning, he headed up the canal bank.

Adam's eyes followed. "I've missed him."

"He's missed you, too.... You don't seem your usual self today, except with Andrew. Is something wrong?"

"Well...I...You've talked with Elias. Has he told you about my short comings?" His hands in his pockets, he looked questioningly at Mr. Charles.

"He mentioned that he's been doing all of the necessary trading. Sounds to me like you have a problem, but then, sometimes problems have a way of taking care of themselves."

"How's that?"

"The freight boat that was supposed to be for sale never became available."

"Good. Then I haven't let you down."

"That depends," Mr. Charles said, a small worry line creasing his brow.

Adam felt his stomach churn. "On what does it depend?"

"I did purchase a boat."

"Oh!"

"It's a mix between a freight boat and a packet boat, a lot like Ralph's boat here. They call it a line boat. With it, no actual trading will be necessary. We'll set firm prices with the Forwarding Agents who do the collecting in Piqua for the contracted loads." Mr. Charles cleared his throat. He looked to the top of the bank where young Andrew was again becoming visible.

Adam's eyes followed Mr. Charles' line of vision.

"Is our Gentleman's Agreement still good?" Mr. Charles asked.

"It is, but what will we haul?"

"We'll bring people traveling, customers and new settlers into the territory. You'll be hauling the people, their belongings, even their wagons."

"That, I can do!" Adam said without reservation.

"Great!" Mr. Charles offered his hand.

Even as Adam shook his hand he already envisioned the travels and the interesting stories he might soon hear. *Helping to bring new settlers,* he thought. *Sounds great!* He felt better already.

CHAPTER 3
Early April, 1840
The New Ohio

Early the next April, when the frozen canal had melted enough for boats to travel, Adam stood at the bow of *The New Ohio* and officially became Captain Adam. *Can it be only five months ago?* he thought as he watched the hoagie lead the mules on the canal bank pulling his boat. The mild lapping of the water against the front and sides of the newly painted boat, and the rope creaking were the only sounds heard.

"Come on, you two. It's a nice day. Pull," said Jim as he sat on the mule closest to the canal.

Laboriously, the animals pulled their load north. Having left Cincinnati late the day before, it would be another day and a half before they reached Piqua. The boat was heavily loaded carrying new settlers and their belongings. Two Conestoga wagons sat on either side of the roofed mid-section.

It was early, only past daybreak. Steam from the animals' nostrils filled the air in puffs as they walked the towpath. The settlers, nine in all, were just beginning to stir.

The Bruckner family consisted of a father, mother, a boy of about ten, a girl of seven, and another small boy nearing three years old.

The Bruckeners had been the first to pay their fee and to be loaded on. Having come across the mountains late last fall they had taken the National Road to Wheeling, and come down the Ohio River to Cincinnati. They had been forced to spend the winter in Cincinnati and were most anxious to be on their way.

The other family, the Zirkles, included a man, only a few years older than Adam, his wife, and her father and mother. They had been traveling the Ohio River and had reached Cincinnati only three days before Adam arrived. A broker had paid their fees early.

The ten-year-old Bruckner boy, his black hair unruly, and sleep still in his eyes, was the first to crawl from under a wagon and make his way forward to Adam. "My name's Thomas," he said rubbing his left eye with his fist. "What's yours?" he asked, still wearing the clothes he'd had on the day before.

"Captain Adam," he answered. The title still sounded strange to him.

"We're going to a new land to start a new life," the boy said as he stretched.

"Do you want to go?"

The boy shrugged his shoulders. "Pa says it's the only way we'll ever be able to have land of our own."

"Is he a farmer?"

"No. He's a blacksmith."

"That's right, son," said the man who'd come up behind his boy and had the same dark, unruly-looking hair. "We'd like a place of our own to make a new start. Back home there's too many rules, too much politics, and too many people. A man needs his space."

"Where is back home?" Adam asked curiously.

"Philadelphia."

"That's in Pennsylvania," young Thomas added.

The father, also wearing yesterday's clothing, smiled as he rested his right hand on the boy's left shoulder. His wife, small-boned and short, came to stand beside them. She held a round tin, seven inches high and ten inches across, in her rough red hands.

"Do you want some bread?" she asked the members of her family. "John and Mary Catherine are still asleep."

"I do," said Thomas.

His mother set the tin on a trunk and opened the lid. "Would you like some, Captain Adam?"

"Thank you, Mrs. Bruckner." Adam said taking the chunk of brown bread she handed to him.

"Can I cook some potatoes and beans for this evening?" she asked.

"You can start your evening meal on our cast iron stove. There is a turn-around where we can pull over for awhile in mid-afternoon. You can finish the cooking over the bonfire," Adam told her.

"The children will need a hot meal then. I will make enough for everyone." Looking back toward their wagon she said, "They are starting to wake." She turned and headed in the direction of the smaller wagon.

"Have you been to a place called Berlin?" the father asked.

"I have, a few years back," Adam answered. "Is that where you're going?"

"I have two cousins that have settled there. They are expecting us," he said. The man shoved his hands into his pockets. "What's it like?"

"A thick forest. The canal is going to go through that area. Two years ago, only a few people lived near the fort."

"My cousins tell me the land is rich, and more people will be coming."

"The land is rich, and I've heard rumors that the town is growing."

The worried look on the man's face began to lessen. "Then it'll be a good place to settle," he said aloud, his fears visibly diminishing.

"It'll grow for sure, being on the canal route," Adam assured him further. "And there is always need for a good blacksmith. They will be glad to have you."

The next morning it was the clucking of two hens being chased by Mary Catherine, the eight-year-old Bruckner girl, who awoke Leo Zirkle, who'd slept with his wife on a quilt under their wagon.

Leo sat upright under the high wagon floor, his white, thin hair on the sides and back of his head in total disarray. He ran his hands over the bald spot on the top of his head, then around the hair on his head, finally across his short, sparse mustache, and finished by smoothing his white, two inch-long beard.

The man looked about and chuckled as he watched the dark-haired girl run around barrels and boxes trying to chase the chickens closer to the Bruckner wagon. Leo shook Judith. "Look," he said and pointed toward Mary Catherine.

Slowly Judith, stiff from her night's sleep on the floor of the boat, sat up, plaiting her long brown and grey hair with her fingers. She, too, watched the child momentarily. "Someone should help her," she said.

"I'm on my way," her son-in-law George said as he jumped down from the oval opening in the back of the canvas-covered wagon. He and Theresa, newlyweds, chose to sleep over her parent's heads on the more uncomfortable wagon floor.

Theresa, her long, light-brown hair falling down to her shoulders, stuck her head out of the opening in the back of the wagon from which George had jumped. "Go to the other side, George," she called with laughter bubbling in her voice.

Later that morning Adam saw Theresa and thought of Alese. His heart aching, he turned his face away from her in the direction of Jim, his twelve-year old hoagie, who was nearly finished with his shift. "Jim, my boy, look for a tie-up post in this turn-around," Adam called.

Shortly Jim found a heavily worn post and wrapped the tow rope around it. *The New Ohio* slowed to a stop in the nearly still water. Jim unhitched his tired team from the long, ninety-foot towline. Within fifteen minutes *The New Ohio* could be on its way again, but Adam had promised Mrs. Bruckner a two-hour stop.

For a while Adam helped and watched the settlers. The children energetically ran along the bank while the women put together a hot meal. The men had started a fire. He saw Theresa, and again Alese came to his mind. *Has she gone on to school? What did she do with her time?* He shook himself. *What is the matter with me? Why can't I get her off my mind?*

Deciding to walk off some of his melancholy, he walked along the bank for awhile. *I like this business. It's interesting and sometimes exciting,* he thought.

Turning back toward the busy settlers, he saw the family life and closeness that some of the men and women had together. *That is what is missing in my life, he realized.* His eyes misted as he felt the muscles around his heart tighten, and felt the emptiness in his stomach.

CHAPTER 4
May 1840
Slaves

It was early morning at a dock close to Lock 36 in Hamilton. Adam watched as once again a Conestoga wagon was loaded onto *The New Ohio*. The owner, Mr. Haviland, stood close by, watching intently.

"You will take care of all my cargo inside the wagon?" he asked Captain Adam when finally the wagon was set securely on the boat. "Some of it is very precious; going to my daughter at Piqua," he said. "She's traveling further north with it."

"I'll take care of it. The ride is smooth, and only at the locks do we get gentle bumps. Your daughter will receive it in fine shape," Adam assured him.

By noon at Lock 28 in Franklin, Captain Adam rang the bell announcing his boat's presence and telling the lock-tender he had work to do.

The lock-tender came; the boat went into the lock. Two men on horses rode up, dismounting at the top of the lock. "We're looking for two slaves," the larger of the men said. "They're runaways."

"The woman's a mulatto. The boy, her son, is about ten. She's light, but he isn't." The man held the reins of his horse.

The other man, in a superior tone of voice asked, "Have you seen them?"

"How could we see them?" Adam asked of the slave hunters. "We've been on the canal all morning," Adam squinted up at them through the sun rays.

"There's a law against harboring them," the man said. "We can have you put in jail."

"We haven't seen them, I tell you," Captain Adam said. "Come on board and take a look for yourself."

The two men hesitated as they looked at each other, and then at the seventy-foot-long boat. "What do you think?" the larger man asked the other.

"Let's go on past. He wouldn't let us come on board if he had them."

Without as much as a thank you, sorry, or anything else, the two slave hunters got on their horses and rode away.

The lock tender closed the lock gates, opened the water wicket, and water flowed in.

Leaving the lock behind them, a smile crept across Adam's face. *I was lucky this time*, he thought.

He sat in his cabin at his table eating pieces of fried chicken and bread he'd picked up at Lock 26 in Miamisburg. After eating his fill, he took the basket and rewrapped the bread and chicken, added two tin cups filled with water from his fresh water bucket.

Back at the Haviland wagon he stepped up and placed the basket he'd filled on the seat of the Conestoga wagon, pushed back the canvas curtain, and crawled into it.

He stood still, closed his eyes momentarily and quickly opened them. Now he was able to see inside the darkened wagon. Halfway down, on the right side, huddled against the wall of the wagon sat a woman. Across her face, even in the dimness, Adam could see the ugly scar on her right cheek.

In a hushed voice he said, "I am a friend." The woman's dress was tattered, her dark hair covered by a scarf. Fear showed in her eyes as the dark pupils in their white background darted, searching for her son.

"Luke," the woman said in a loving voice.

A boy, of nearly ten, so black in color he blended, more so than his mamma, into the dark. He inched his way out from under a bench and other stacked furniture that made a tunnel in which the fugitives could hide. Once out from under, he quietly moved to the side of his mamma.

Adam handed the basket of food and water to the woman. "Mr. Haviland has made arrangements for you to ride to Piqua in this wagon. He told me you are running. Your name is Cecei and your boy is Luke?"

"Yes sir. Our master was going to whip Luke fifty times cause he was learning to read and write. It would kill him, sir.

"Did he give you the scar on your cheek?"

"Yes, sir. Last year he wants to sell my Luke. I hid in the field with him for a week. When they found us he did this to me." Her hand touched the scar. "Said he would still sell him when he was ten. His birthday in three months."

"Don't worry about any of that," Adam said. "I'll bring you each a blanket. For now you are safe."

Several hours later, as *The New Ohio* waited behind a freighter to enter the next lock, the same two slave hunters who had stopped them at Lock 28, in Franklin, anxious to get the reward offered for captured slaves, rode up to the tow path.

The larger man, who talked with authority, came to the edge of the boat. "We want to take a look on your boat for those niggers."

"Do you have papers on them?" Adam questioned.

"Right here," the man said as he pulled folded sheets from his jacket pocket and waved them in the air.

Adam walked to the edge of the boat and reached for the papers. "Let me see them."

The men got down off of their horses. The large man handed the papers to Adam.

Adam took his time reading.

Negro Runaways
1 female mulatto negress, light in color, age thirty,
light brown eyes.
Identifying mark: slash on her right cheek. Goes by
the name of Cecei. 54 inches tall

1 male black boy, near ten years, dark brown eyes.
Is son of Cecei. Goes by name of Luke. 48 inches tall. Can read some

Reward *for capture. Contact Kent Colant of Virgina*

Adam handed the papers back to the man. "I haven't seen them. I told you earlier, I have not seen any negroes. What more do you want?" asked Adam.

"We want to take a look."

"I'm not going to let you," Adam said. "This is my boat and you have no right to board her."

"Then we'll have to get the sheriff."

"Let me see your paper allowing you to look for them."

The man again reached back into his jacket pocket and pulled out another paper and handed it to Adam.

"It's a bad day when a man can't have privacy on his own boat." Adam read the paper and handed it back to the man. "Come on board then, as though it will do you any good."

The two men tied their horses to a tree on the far side of the towpath, and then returned. Smugly, while *The New Ohio* was still waiting to enter the lock, they set foot on board.

Arrogantly they started for the front of the boat. "Wait one moment," Adam said. "I will escort you and you will follow me."

"What, and give you time to hide those niggers!"

Adam reached into his jacket pocket and showed them a small pistol. "You will do as I say or you will get off my boat!"

"Oh," the large man said. Then willingly, "Let's do it your way."

"One of my crew will follow us."

"What? Well, all right. Whatever you say," the large man said. The smaller man nodded his head in agreement.

Adam led them to the rear of the boat to his cabin. "I want you to see this and check it out." He waited while they looked under his blankets, looked at the top bunk, and under Adam's bunk where he stored bags. There was no place else for slaves to hide.

They went from there to the first of the wagons on board. He let the men crawl up and look inside the wagon filled with household goods, boxes and a trunk. "No one in there," the smaller man said as the two crawled out and down from the wagon.

Adam let them look inside the barrels on deck, full of nails and canned goods. He also let them look inside the boxes which held bolts of fabric and spools of thread.

From there the men, as Adam looked on, went into the mule stable. They glanced at the wire baskets and buckets and shelves hanging on the upper walls. They seemed satisfied and walked back up the plank.

Against the stable wall leaned a stack of straw for bedding and another stack of hay for feeding. A pitchfork stood close by. The larger man picked it up and with force jabbed it several times into each stack. "Hrumf," he said. "Not in there."

Adam took them around to the tongue of the Haviland wagon. He crawled up and into the wagon himself leading them. His eyes adjusted by the time they were all inside. There was barely room to stand, and since the sides of the wagon bottom were rounded, their balance was not good.

"What's in here?" the smaller man said as he held on to one of the legs of a table turned upside down.

"Be careful," Adam cautioned. "This is Mr. Haviland's wagon and his cargo is precious. Some of these boxes hold china, some glassware. They're for his daughter."

"We don't care who they're for," the large man said.

"You will if you damage any of it. Mr. Haviland will have the sheriff on you." They had moved to the back of the wagon. "Now what else do you need to see in here?" Adam asked.

The two men made motions of looking under the furniture and around the boxes, but space was limited, so they finally gave up.

"Let's get out of here," the large man said.

Once again on the deck the two men were allowed to look under and around the wagons.

"Are you satisfied they are not on my boat?" Adam asked demanding an answer.

"We didn't see them."

"Then get off," Adam said forcefully, "and don't be coming back or I'll personally have the sheriff after you."

The two scrambled off the boat.

Adam went to the rear, to his cabin. "Never did like carrying a gun," he said aloud as he put it in a bag near his bunk.

"You two stay put for a bit until I'm sure those men are gone and we've been through the lock." He pulled a few of his cloth bags further out from under the bunk, giving them more room.

Out on the deck he looked for the two men who were now on their horses. *I knew that opening beneath my bunk would come in handy.*

A smile crossed his face. *Mr. Haviland's precious cargo is safe,* he thought, nodding. A sly look came into his eyes. We may need to use that bunk door again. He rang the bell for the lock-tender. It was their turn to enter.

CHAPTER 5
Early Summer of 1840
Summer Wedding

Adam and Otto sat on a long bench at the back of the parlor with two other wedding guests. He and Otto had met two days earlier when Otto boarded *The New Ohio* at Cincinnati. They had become fast friends.

"Come with me tomorrow to my cousin's wedding," Otto said, inviting him.

"I don't know them," Adam said.

"You will after the wedding, and they'd like having you. Anyone who's my friend is their friend. We're that kind of family."

So Adam had come to the ceremony with his new friend.

The bride, dressed in an ivory silk-taffeta, floor-length gown, stood in the doorway at the top of the narrow stairs. Her full skirt that covered many crinolines and a tight bodice emphasized her small waist. Her skirts swayed gently.

A woman wearing a long, frilly, rose-colored gown began to play a soft tune on the pump organ. Voices of the guests quieted. Heads turned as the groom and the best man came in from a side room.

Adam glanced again at the top of the stairs. In front of the bride stood a young lady dressed in a yellow, satin dress with lace gloves that went to her elbows. A small yellow satin hat covered the top of her head. Her long dark curls fell loosely about her shoulders.

As the young lady's toe touched the second step, the processional march began. Again all heads turned. They watched her until she was nearly halfway down the steps. At that time, the bride started to descend the steps.

Adam saw only the young lady dressed in yellow. At the bottom of the stairs she turned to face the guests. His heart stopped. He had thought it looked like her. It was Alese!

He felt the nudging before Otto asked, "Quite a looker, eh?"

Adam nodded. "I know her," he said.

He thought back to the day when he first met her on the canal boat, and then to later, when for the first time he truly noticed her. The scene had played over in his mind many times. He could still hear that kitchen door close as she went to help her mother get the grape desert.

The short minister stood tall, dressed in black except for the wide white collar around his neck. He cleared his throat. "Family and friends we are gathered here together with MaryAnn and Dominic on this joyous occasion. Standing up for them while this young couple make their vows are Alese Reed and Orville Weaver."

Alese Reed, her name echoed in his head. He barely heard the rest of the marriage ceremony.

"How do you know her?" Otto asked Adam.

The ceremony over, Adam rubbed his forehead in his dilemma of what to tell to Otto. He knew only that she affected him like no other. "I'll tell you later," he said. As the guests stood up and began to mill about, he headed toward her.

He stood quietly to the side as she talked animatedly with two young ladies. Noticing him, the two young women moved on to visit with others, and he moved closer.

Just as she was within arm's length, a little girl, wearing a flowered dress with a wide ribbon around her waist took hold of Alese's hand and pulled her away.

"Come see," the girl said as she led her out through the front door.

Alese had seemed not to notice Adam who walked to the side window. In the pane was glass, not the standard greased paper. Adam himself had helped to make it possible to have glass. He'd carried shipments of it north, on his boat from Cincinnati.

Except for the small waves in the glass, Adam could clearly see the hundred year old oak trees that nearly hid the tall windmill from the road, and even see the wheel of the windmill slowly turning in the breeze. To the right of the windmill was the barn.

Otto had shown the barn to him earlier. It stood two stories high. The top story had a mow for straw and hay. Underneath, on one side, work horses were housed. On the other side were bins for grain storage. In the center there was room enough for the plow, harrow, farm wagons, harnesses, and other small field equipment.

This family is not poor. No one I know has glass windows in their home, and a barn the size of this one, he thought.

The land, over one hundred acres, was good, and most of it was cleared. Adam had seen it many times from the canal that ran through the back of the property.

From the window he saw Alese sitting on the porch steps with the little girl. They were talking and laughing while playing with two small kittens.

Deciding, he walked to the front door, opened it and set foot on the porch.

"Adam." The look of recognition followed by the smile on her face increased the confidence he felt.

"Hello, Alese."

"How are you, Adam?"

"Surprised to see you," he said.

"I'm surprised to see you."

"What's your name?" he asked the girl as he sat down beside them.

"Nettie," the girl said. Alese handed her kitten to Adam.

"The mama cat had only two babies this time," Nettie said, handing her kitten to Adam, too. "See."

Awkwardly he held both of the kittens, one in each hand, and looked at them carefully. "I think they miss their mama," he said and handed the kittens back to each of the girls.

"I'll take them back to the summer kitchen," said Nettie as she reached for the one that Alese now held.

"I saw you with MaryAnn's cousin," Alese said.

"How do you know his cousin?" he asked.

"I met her at Oberlin College. We became best of friends from the moment we met. They asked me to stand up for them."

"How do you know her cousin?" Alese asked in turn.

"Otto's a passenger on my boat...Mr. Charles' boat, that is. Like you and MaryAnn, we became fast friends. He thought I might enjoy the wedding, especially the food and the music."

"Are you enjoying it?" she asked, her dark brown eyes looking up at him.

"So far. Especially, since I saw you in that pretty yellow dress."

"Thank you," she said. "I like your captain's jacket, too. What do your passengers call you?"

"Captain Adam."

"Suits you," she said smiling. Want to take a little walk?"

He nodded, and they both stood up. "How's school going?"

"It's hard, but I like it. Mr. Charles is helping me with the expenses."

"He's a decent and generous man," Adam said. "He's put me where I am."

"Not from what I hear," Alese said as she walked toward the young apple orchard. Adam walked beside her. "Mr. Charles has nothing but respect for your abilities, and, of course, Andrew thinks of you as the big brother who can do anything."

Adam laughed, embarrassed by the praise. "That's only because we don't spend that much time together."

"Andrew would love to help you on the boat," she said.

"And would you like to be my stable hand? So far I don't have any restrictions about girls working on my boat," he teased.

She laughed. She reached out, touching the leaves and small branches of the trees. "I've been told these trees were planted by a man who carried little seedlings in his backpack. I wonder if they truly were." She looked up at him, "what do you think?"

"I heard of him too. They called him Johnny Appleseed. He walked a great deal of this country doing just that. So, maybe they were planted by him."

As they walked she lifted her long dress to step over a log. "How do you like being captain of your own boat?"

"I never dreamed I'd ever do anything like it. Sometimes I think it's not possible that I'm a Captain of a canal boat. I like it, but I miss having a family around."

"As a captain couldn't you have a wife and a couple of children with you?"

"I've seen a few families on boats. I'm not sure how they manage. There isn't a great deal of room on the boats."

It was then that Nettie came, half skipping and half running toward them. "It's time to eat," she said. "I was sent to tell you to come in now."

Canal Culvert

PART FOUR

CHAPTER 1
Early October 1842
A Letter

On this Wednesday afternoon, like most others, the canal boat traffic was heavy. A hint of chill was in the fall air as the canal boats lined up behind each other. Andrew, now 14, sometimes worked for Adam. He stood by as they waited in line to go through the lock.

Once through the lock, and eventually into a short feeder, *The New Ohio* stopped close at the edge of the bank behind the packet boat which carried the mail.

"I can see the General Store," Andrew said as he helped to set the plank to the bank. Stone steps were embedded into the bank wall leading up to the pathway three feet above.

The town's all out, and wait'n for news, thought Adam as he saw people gather above on the edge of the bank.

Adam's passengers, the Coxes, who owned the General Store, stood on the flat rooftop of the rear cabin section of *The New Ohio*, anxious to see their friends. Norman Cox held tight to the wide brim of his black hat waving to the townspeople.

"Norman," Adam said, "Time to help Mrs. Cox down to the deck."

Barbara descended the side ladder with him helping. Her bonnet ties hung loose in front of her full gathered skirt. At five feet she stood six inches shorter than her husband.

They had ridden the canal boat south, almost to Cincinnati to attend her father's funeral. Before they returned they purchased supplies for their general store located in the front part of their home. Inside a crate tagged for them were sets of hardware, small tools and many bolts of fabric.

At the top of the bank Adelaide met them.

"Let's hurry," Barbara said. "We've got customers coming."

"Did you scrub the seats in the outhouse?" Norman asked Adelaide, Barbara's niece, who had come north to help her aunt. Adelaide nodded, quickly hugged Barbara, and rushed to check that all was ready.

Before Barbara followed, she visually checked to see if the enameled basin was on the wooden bench and a clean cotton towel hung on a nail at the side of the building. She saw the fresh chunk of lye soap and the bucket of clean water ready for anyone who wanted to wash. Automatically she looked toward the pump. The shiny tin cup hung on a hook beckoning to the thirsty.

Passengers of the packet boat followed a less steep path up to the General Store. Norman and Barbara arrived ahead of them, and greeted their customers on the front porch of the store.

Inside, a small crowd gathered around the display of baskets.

"I never saw one like this," a young blonde woman said.

"Neither have I. It's about the same size as the one your mother has, isn't it" The older man beside her asked.

The woman picked up the round basket, turning it while her finger traced the flow of the woven pattern. "Hers is not nearly as nice, but I want this one for us," she said and handed it to the gray-haired man. "That smaller one is the one I had in mind for Mama."

"We'll take both," he said to Norman who stood behind the counter.

Women in long-sleeved dresses purchased items. Others went from the store empty handed. One of the young men, dressed in clean, but worn clothes bought a newly baked loaf of bread. After paying for it, he tore a chunk from it, and put it in his mouth.

"We have some butter, just churned. "Adelaide said when she saw him. "Would you like some? There's no charge."

"Yeah," he said.

Adelaide used the butter paddle to spread a nice-sized pat on an ironstone saucer. The man pulled a folding knife out of his pocket and spread the butter on the first portion of the loaf. While eating, he slowly walked toward the door.

Norman whispered in Adelaide's ear. "He's just about the right age for you."

"Now, Uncle Norman, I'm not ready to find a man!" She said, protesting too much.

It was then that Captain Osgood from the packet boat stood in front of the counter.

"Is there a lady here by the name of Adelaide?" He grinned as he looked at her.

"You know there is," Adelaide said laughing.

"There is a letter for you," he handed it to her. "See you the next time through," he said. He winked, and wore a wide grin as he left, herding his passengers back down to his boat. They had been there less than an hour.

Barbara and Norman chatted as they restocked, swept up bread crumbs from the floor, and rearranged the disarray.

Adelaide stood holding her letter. Adam, seeing it in her hand, remembered that he had not had time to read the letter he'd received from Mr. Waite from Maumee. "We must be on our way," he said to the Coxes as he made a final purchase and headed down to *The New Ohio* with Andrew at his heels.

Standing on the deck, Adam reached for his gold pocket watch, opened it, looked at the face, fingered the gold ring that had been his mother's, closed the watch cover, and reached into his side pocket for the letter. Carefully he loosened the wax seal and read.

September 1842
Dear Adam,

It has been quite some time since I have heard from you. I need to bring to your attention that, things are changing in Maumee.

Your properties are intact, and your rental monies are growing. However, there has been an offer on your two parcels which overlook the river.

I understand you are now Captain of *The New Ohio*. The inland water system is not yet totally finished, but we have a canal system here that is quite enviable. Consider coming back to your roots. The sight of your face would do my heart good.

Until your wishes are made clear regarding your property, nothing will be done.

I am looking forward to either seeing you or receiving a note from you.

Sincerely,
And in friendship,

David Waite

Slowly Adam folded the letter and placed it back into his pocket. *Being a canal boat captain at Maumee would be a challenge,* he thought.

He motioned for the mule skinner to move on.

CHAPTER 2
Mid-October 1842
A Return to Maumee

"It's too early to close the boat down for the season," Adam said to Mr. Charles.

"Yes, it is." Mr. Charles agreed. "Why do you want to?"

The weather was beautiful. Autumn leaves had started to fall, padding the earth for the winter. Soon snow and ice would be covering that padding.

Adam had never told Mr. Charles about his background. He'd taken him at face value. Now Adam needed to tell him.

The two were out in the barn, looking at the seed bin. "You haven't yet told me what is bothering you," Mr. Charles said.

"Let's sit down," Adam said. "It's a long story, and I want to tell you all of it." They sat on a long wooden bench.

"When I first met you, I was a farm boy. I lived with my aunt and uncle who took me in when I was four. My parents were from Maumee and were both dead." He got up and started to pace.

"It was a month or so later, after our trip to Piqua where we met you, when Jake came to see me. His mother wanted me to go with them to Maumee to visit her brother who'd been injured."

"I felt I owed Jake that much, since it was my idea to go to Piqua and he'd gotten shot. Anyway, I'd not been to Maumee since I was a child. I was curious to see it. I wondered if I'd remember anything." He leaned against the seed bin.

"I told my aunt and uncle that I thought I ought to go. They agreed. That's when my aunt showed me some papers I'd had with me when I'd first come to them. One was a letter telling them I had some monies coming from my parents." He went over and sat beside Mr. Charles again who was listening attentively.

"No one knew how much. They had never inquired. So Jake and his mother and I took their buggy and drove to Maumee."

"How were the roads?"

"Not good, but passable. We were lucky not to have had any rain."

"While we were there I went to see my parent's good friend who's a solicitor. He's the one who sent the papers with me. It was quite an experience. He didn't know for sure if I was alive, so he was shocked to see me. He had invested some of my monies in property and kept others in cash."

Adam leaned over, picked up a piece of wheat straw and began tearing little narrow slivers down the length of it.

"There must have been a lot of money."

"Yes, there was cash and three different pieces of land, as well as the home where I was born. There was also a piece of property that the solicitor had purchased in the canal Black Swamp area. He'd thought that it would be a good investment, too.

"I guess I wasn't the only one then," Mr. Charles said.

"No, you weren't," Adam agreed, and went on with his story.

"During the time I was there I sold the business property, but held on to the other three parcels in Maumee. I still haven't decided what to do with the Black Swamp land along the canal."

He looked at Mr. Charles. "That brings you up to the present. I have received a letter from Mr. Waite, my solicitor. He'd like for me to come to Maumee to see about my properties. I'd like to do that soon, before the winter weather boxes us in. I plan to stay until early spring, before the ground thaws, hoping to be back to start the season with the boat." Again, Adam was pacing.

"I'd like to sleep on it, Adam," Mr. Charles said. "You will stay with us won't you? I know Alese and Andrew would like you to. I would, too." He got up and held out his hand. "We still have an agreement, but that doesn't mean we can't make changes."

Later, after the evening meal, and after Andrew had talked and listened to Adam, he and Alese sat together in the parlor. She seemed even more beautiful to him than he remembered.

As she was one of the very first women to attend college in the area, he was proud of her. She worked daily in Piqua, doing bookwork for the Forwarding and Commission Merchants House for the entire canal system. She was a valuable citizen. When she stayed in town during the week she rented an upstairs room from a maiden lady. Weekends she spent on the farm, again doing book work for Mr. Charles to lower her financial debt to him.

"Why do you want to go for that long?" Alese asked.

"Those properties are not out in the wild, but right in the Maumee area. I need to understand what is going on in Maumee and what would be best for me to do with them. Would it upset you if I stay awhile?" he asked.

Blushing, Alese said, "It's so far away, and we don't see much of each other." She hesitated, "I'd feel better with you closer."

"While I'm there, I'll keep that in mind," he said smiling at her, and added. "I'd like to see more of you, too."

That is how they left it.

In the early morning Adam and Mr. Charles sat in the kitchen. "Adam, I'd like for you to stay on the boat another month. That will still give you time to get to Maumee before winter sets in." He put his fork on his plate. "Coming back early before the ice melts on the canal would be fine. You could take up as Captain again, if you haven't changed your mind about what you want to do."

"I haven't. That is agreeable." They shook on it.

CHAPTER 3
Late November 1842
Named for a Friend

The cold air rushed through the stagecoach's leather-covered windows. Under the padded bench sat foot warmers filled with coals. They had been hot when the coach left the last stop.

Adam was glad he had chosen not to ride his horse and had ridden in the coach instead, letting Sam trail behind. *It will be another three hours before we reach Maumee,* he thought as he put his head back, trying to nap.

The road's roughness made that nearly impossible. Finally, he shifted his position until he was at an angle. He put one of his smaller bags behind his head, pulled up his coat collar, and snuggled into the corner. He felt more comfortable. The other two men in the coach were not interested in conversation. Finally he slept.

Mr. Waite, a wide smile on his face, met Adam when the stage coach stopped at the Maumee destination. The air felt colder in Maumee than it had when he'd left Piqua, where he had dry-docked the boat for the winter. Adam mentioned it to Mr. Waite as he untied Sam from the coach.

"It is colder," the older man said. "We're quite a bit further north. Our winter is ahead of yours. I brought the buggy. You can tie your horse behind." They got into the buggy. "In the back of my house is a clean stable with straw, hay and oats. He'll be comfortable there."

"Sam hasn't had much of a rest since we left. He wasn't bearing a load, but he had to keep up. At times that stage moves out."

"Sam's an unusual name for a horse."

"I named him for a friend who goes by Samuel. The man is trustworthy and dependable." Adam looked at Mr. Waite. "Just like you!"

A look of surprise, and then a smile appeared on Mr. Waite's face. "Never had a horse named after me before. Kind of like it," he chuckled, "though Sam doesn't look much like me."

"Nope. He's got two extra legs. You'd look funny with that many." They both laughed.

Two weeks later Adam and Mr. Waite rode in the buggy up to Toledo.

"Canals are the cheapest and safest mode of transportation," Mr. Waite said as they stood near Lake Erie on the bank of the Wabash & Erie Canal. "Would you consider being a Captain on this canal? It'll run all the way to the Ohio River, though the Connection to the Miami & Erie Extension won't be finished for another year."

"There's so much I need to consider in this next year," Adam said turning up his coat collar to ward off the cold chill coming off the lake.

They rode back in silence, listening to the clip clop of horse's hooves and trying to keep warm.

"I think I picked the wrong time to come. It's so cold."

"Ah, but it gets warm and sunshiny in the early summer. The lake is great for fishing. Do you fish?"

"I'm Captain of a boat, but I've never fished. I've seen people fishing along the canal. They seem to enjoy themselves."

"Fishing in the canal? What else do they do in the canal?"

"Kids go swimming behind the boats sometimes. In the winter, people ice skate on the canal, sometimes from one town to another. They also collect ice off of the turn-arounds and from the canal. They pack it in straw or sawdust and store it in buildings until spring. If it isn't used, the ice is hauled down to Cincinnati and sold."

"Do you do the hauling?"

"Ice is one thing I've never hauled." He looked at Mr. Waite with a twinkle in his eye. "Maybe I should take some back with me. What do you think?"

"I'll let you know next summer if we still have any." Mr. Waite said chuckling.

CHAPTER 4
December 1842
A New Venture

"Mr. Waite, does your housekeeper cook for you like that every night?" Adam asked as he stood in front of the fireplace warming his backside.

"Call me Samuel," Mr. Waite said.

"Yes, sir."

"Adam," Samuel said, "your parents and I were the best, and the closest of friends. Had they lived, do you think you'd be calling me Mr. Waite or sir?"

Adam, embarrassed, answered, "Maybe you'd be Uncle Samuel?"

"Now that's more like it," he said. "And to answer your question, yes, she always makes a good evening meal for me."

"You're a lucky man."

"I am indeed."

"I think I've finally gotten warm," Adam said as he moved away from the fireplace. "I've seen most of Maumee. It's so different from the Piqua area. Do you like living here?"

"I'm satisfied," Samuel said, "my business is here, and I like being near the water. It took a little time for me to get used to the length of the seasons, and the port activity, but now I enjoy all of it."

Adam sat in one of the arm chairs in front of the fire place. "I don't know if I'd like living here. I'd miss my family, and my friends, and I'm not that fond of the cold weather," he said. "Of course we have cold weather at home, too," Adam said. "Maybe, it's just that I've never been away from home this long."

"That could be part of it, Samuel said. "Adam, do you have a lady friend in Piqua?"

Adam nodded. "Her name's Alese." His voice sounded brighter. "I care about her, and I think she feels the same about me."

"Have you made a commitment?"

"Not spoken, though I've not met anyone else that I care for more."

"Tell me about her."

Adam told Samuel of their first meeting. "She's now through Oberlin College, and during the week works as a bookkeeper in a Canal Commission Merchant House in Piqua. On weekends she keeps Mr. Charles' accounts up to date."

"She's a busy lady."

"She is that! Speaking of the Canal Commission Merchant House, reminds me that I wanted to ask you about warehouses. Do you think my two pieces of property by the river might make a nice location for a warehouse?"

For a moment Samuel said nothing. "You amaze me, Adam."

"Why is that?"

"Just a few days before you arrived I was discussing just such a possibility with a banker friend of mine. In fact, it's his bank that holds your account."

"And what did he say?"

"He thought that it was a good idea, especially since the property will be close to the canal and by the river," Samuel said. "What's more, when the sidecut is through, your land will be within access of some of the lake traffic, as well."

"Then you think it would be a profitable enterprise?"

"Most certainly!"

"What would it cost me to build a warehouse?" Adam asked. "I still have most of the money left from the building I sold."

"If you have no strong feelings about the house your parent's lived in, it could be sold for a tidy sum. It's in a good location."

"Would the money from the property we sold earlier, and now my parent's home cover the cost of building the warehouse?"

"It should come close. However, you'll need cash to get the warehouse started and to hire help," Samuel said. "Would you oversee the management of the warehouse or would you hire that done?"

"Whew, this is all moving so fast. Let me give these things some thought," Adam said and then added, "Since you're more familiar with costs, maybe together we could put some figures down on paper?"

"We sure can, my boy. I'm thrilled for you. What a venture this could be!" The excitement sounded in Samuel's voice. "You're so much like your father."

Time was passing fast. Christmas was now only two weeks away, and Adam's family and Alese were definitely on his mind. He had never missed a Christmas with his aunt and uncle.

In the next day or so, after he and Samuel had gone over proposed expenses for what seemed like the tenth time, Adam decided to go ahead and have the warehouse built. Some of the expenses were still not certain, but Adam had been frugal and saved most of his money from having worked on the canal boat. He felt he would be able to swing the costs.

Samuel, after some discussion, agreed to oversee the building of the warehouse which would start as soon as the spring thaw and sufficient water drainage would allow. They figured that it would take until the early fall of the next year to finish the warehouse, as there was much other building going on.

Adam appreciated the length of time. *In another six months I'll be able to save more money,* he thought.

Samuel looked at him. "The bank can lend you start-up money. You might find you'll need a certain amount for things that we haven't accounted for." Samuel had a smile on his face when he said, "You indeed, are a lucky young man to be able to start a venture like this." He double checked some figures. "I'll be glad to help you out financially, too, with whatever you need. Another possibility that you might consider," he said, "to bring in extra money, would be to start a cooperage within the warehouse making barrels for shipment of goods."

"That never crossed my mind," Adam said. You're helping me in so many ways."

"You're my only family, Adam. I love you like a son."

"The feeling is mutual, Samuel. One thing, though, and I don't mean to offend your hospitality, but I'm thinking about heading home for Christmas."

"I can't say I blame you. If I had a family I'd want to be with them as well.

"You're part of my family. Come home with me for the holidays. Your business shouldn't suffer too much."

"I'm not sure I'd be welcome."

"You would be. You can meet Alese and her family, and Mr. Charles and his wife, too. Aunt Trudy and Uncle Joseph would love to see you. What do you say?"

"When you put it that way how can I refuse? Shall we start day after tomorrow if we can get a coach? Do you want Sam to follow along behind?"

Adam nodded affirming his verbal, "Yes."

"Then let's do it." Samuel said as he walked over to Adam, and gave him an affectionate hug. "You have filled an empty place in my heart, and in my life."

CHAPTER 5
June 1843
Land Money Squandered

Spring had arrived, and *The New Ohio* was once again making its way up and down the Canal, but only as far north as the Piqua area. There had been many problems extending the canal from Piqua and connecting it to a further point north, past the St. Marys Reservoir.

To continue the canal, the St. Marys Reservoir water supply was absolutely necessary. The land used for the reservoir had been taken by the state with the promise to pay the farmers a given sum. The farmers, however, had not been paid, and the reservoir was filling with water. The farmers, in need of the money to relocate and to live on, were frustrated and bitter. They were becoming irate, and were threatening to damage the reservoir if they weren't paid.

Adam enjoyed the early warm weather, but he felt ill at ease because of the problems at the reservoir. Money always seemed to be a problem. It was no different now. He knew that the farmers' threat to cut the reservoir banks was the beginning of the state's problem.

That was why on a regular schedule, whenever he had a chance to talk with people in the know, or whenever a paper was available Adam kept himself abreast of the situation.

Today he was able to pick up a newspaper with the full account. He took time out, while *The New Ohio* continued on its way, to read the newspaper.

> *On the 3rd of May, 1843 a meeting was held in Celina. It was decided that Benjamin Linzee should go to the head of the Board of Public Works and lay the grievances of the St. Marys Reservoir landowners before it. They wanted and were entitled to their money.*

Adam had heard several times that the monies from the state, due the landowners had been squandered by trusted bank officers and speculators. He didn't blame the landowners for threatening to let water off their flooded reservoir properties. After all, it was their land, and they were entitled to payment. It wasn't like they had a choice in letting the state have the land for the reservoir. And Mr. Linzee had explained the whole situation clarifying their position.

Adam read on.

> *After Mr. Linzee talked with them the monies still did not come through. On May 15, 1843 at 7 a.m. over 100 people with shovels, spades and wheelbarrows assembled at the old Beaver Channel, the strongest place on the bank of the reservoir. The people were ready to cut the bank to let the water off their land.*
>
> *It took the land owners a day and a half to complete the job. They dug six feet below the water level where they'd made a flimsy barricade to hold the water back until they were finished. When the barricade was opened, the waters hurled 50 yards down to the land below.*
>
> *It would take six weeks before the leaking waters would subside.*
>
> *Arrest warrants were issued for all who had assisted in the cutting of the bank. Thirty-four of the warrants went to county officers, including one to Judge Benjamin Linzee. In*

*the end the grand jury let the matter rest and the state paid
$17,000 to repair the damages.*

Adam smiled. "Serves the state right," he said to himself and
shuffled the pages he'd read, putting them down beside the bench he
was sitting on. He laid his head back against the wall.

It was a warm, sunny day. Adam's mind wandered back to when
he first heard that a canal system might solve some of Ohio's
problems. He wondered what General Washington, who was first to
suggest a canal, would think if he could see all the problems and
advantages his suggestion had started.

Once more Adam thought about the farmers and how the state
flooded their land. He could not help himself; he was behind the
farmers one-hundred percent. "I guess I haven't changed much," he
said aloud; "I'm still a farmer at heart."

CHAPTER 6
Late October 1845
A Wedding Celebration

A bright orange pumpkin sat in the center of the sideboard. From the pumpkin, running the full length on either side, lay twigs of red and orange bittersweet. Trays of silverware, cups and glasses covered the one side. The other held sliced breads, muffins and rolls.

Boards had been put in the dining room table to open it as long as possible. High backed-chairs surrounded the table, which was covered in a white cloth, place-settings awaiting.

Many aromas blended together throughout the house, but in the warm kitchen there were chicken, turkey and dressing, sweet potatoes, mashed potatoes, carrots, jars of pickles, and bowls of apple sauce soon to be eaten.

In her upstairs bedroom Alese looked out the window. Her mother, coming up behind, slipped her arms around Alese's waist. "Are you having second thoughts?"

"Life will never be the same again," Alese said, slowly turning to look at her mother. A tear sparkled in her right eye. "I worry about you."

"You shouldn't. You're only going to be a quarter of a mile from here, and Andrew will be here most of the time."

"I know." She kissed her mother's cheek. "Maybe I do have the jitters."

"You've loved him from first sight, when you were on that canal boat. You still feel the same, don't you?"

Yes. It's just such a big step, but I'm ready." She reached for the hem of the ivory taffeta bridal dress that lay on her bed. "I love you, Mother."

"And I love you. Be happy."

"We will be." She turned so that her mother could close the small round covered buttons with the small loops that ran from the center back of her neckline to below her waist.

Downstairs in the study, Adam paced back and forth. *I've never been this nervous before,* he thought.

His Uncle Joseph stood in front of the window. "Adam," he said, "this is what you want to do, isn't it?"

"Yes," Adam said, wringing his sweating hands. He had on his new, black broadcloth coat and silk vest. His beaver top hat lay on the end table by the leather couch.

As he stood beside his Uncle Joseph, his feet hurting because of his new shoes, he looked out the window, watching Samuel get out of the buggy that Andrew had driven to Piqua. *Those two are some of my favorite people,* he thought as a smile covered his features.

Joseph, seeing the change, said, "Now that's more like it, son. This is a happy occasion. I'll go see if everyone is ready."

The door did not quite close as Joseph left. Adam went to close it. Wondering if all the guests were there, he quietly walked out of the door to the edge of the parlor where he stood partially hidden by a large fern on a pedestal.

His Aunt Trudy, his cousins: little Freda, Seth, and Marcus, sat on the first row of chairs. Behind Trudy sat her good friend and neighbor Marta, Frank, her husband, and their son, Ben in the middle of the row. Annie and Zach sat close at the end of the row. *Zach looks happy,* Adam thought.

With surprise he saw Natt standing beside Jake. Mary Ann's husband stood in front of the window, talking with Captain Elias.

Mr. Charles and his wife, Elizabeth, welcomed Samuel at the front door. They had become good friends since Samuel's first trip to Piqua.

Alese's mother, Margaret, stood at the bottom of the open stairway dressed in a soft emerald, floor-length dress. *She looks so pretty,* thought Adam. Quickly he turned to go back into the study.

Minutes later, he and Andrew stood together in the parlor as the soft music from the pump organ began.

He smiled at his Aunt Trudy. He loved her so. If he had had to have someone to take his mother's place, he was quite happy it had been her.

She had not ridden on a canal boat until the day before. Her family had gotten on the boat at the feeder in Sidney. The few hours wait at Lockport didn't seem to bother her. "And the best part is your wedding," she'd said holding his face in her hands before kissing and holding him tightly after she arrived.

It is the best part, thought Adam as the music stopped. All heads turned toward the stairway.

Mary Ann, dressed in a soft, fern-green gown, was several steps down from the landing. She carried a small bouquet of Shasta Daisies and English Ivy.

At the top of the landing, Alese stood ready to come down the steps. Her dark hair hung in long loose curls under the veil of ivory net.

Her long ivory dress of taffeta gently rocked as the many crinolines underneath moved. Delicate taffeta and lace covered the bodice from the high neckline collar to her small waist. Lacy puffed sleeves ran down to wide wrist bands, closed with a line of small buttons.

Adam watched her as she walked down to the bottom step. *Mother's gold cameo locket and chain are perfect for the dress,* he thought.

Alese adjusted her bouquet of Shasta Dasies and the trailing English Ivy that lay gracefully on top of white lace streamers.

She is so beautiful, he thought, not moving until she turned his way with a smile and a look of love in her brown eyes. His heart melted. *She will be mine forever,* was all he could think.

The four stood together in front of the minister; Mary Ann beside Alese, and Andrew beside Adam.

"Dearly beloved, on this special day, we are gathered here," is all that Adam heard until the minister asked Alese if she would take this man.

"I will," she said, her voice strong and firm as she looked at him.

"Will you take this woman…"

"I will," Adam said, getting lost in her eyes.

"Do you have the ring?" The minister asked Adam.

"Yes," he nearly stuttered as he reached for his gold watch and pulled it from his pocket. Unclipping the chain he took his mother's ring from it. Returning the watch to his pocket….

"Repeat after me," the minister said. "With this ring, I thee wed."

Adam held the ring at the tip of her fingers and slipped it onto the third finger of her left hand. "With this ring, I thee wed."

"I now pronounce you man and wife. You may kiss the bride," the minister said.

Adam, full of the love he felt for her, kissed her softly on her lips. "I love you," he whispered.

CHAPTER 7
Mid-July 1849
Cholera

In the spring of 1849 the thaw came and with it, swollen rivers filled with ice and debris. A severe drought followed. In the town of Minster, water was stagnant. In the blistering heat, sewage lay in shallow ditches.

By mid-July houseflies and birds were few and nearly non-existent. People began to be sick.

A person might feel ill in the morning. By noon he might have diarrhea, cramps and vomiting. By evening he might have died. His neighbor might have been walking down the street talking. Suddenly he might start to wobble, as though he'd had too much to drink, and then fall to the street dead.

At an emergency meeting in Piqua, Adam looked at the unsmiling faces of the people. Sadness showed deep in their eyes.

"It's a plague," someone whispered. The room went still except for the nodding of heads. Fear moved openly about the room.

"I've seen it myself," said an old man. He hopelessly threw up his arms. "A body can be hearty in the morning. By evening he'll be frightfully pale and close to death."

✿ ✿ ✿

Adam knew the situation was bad. He remembered early last week, when the normal excitement he'd anticipated, with the arrival of *The New Ohio* at a village, was missing.

The lock tender had called out warningly. We're struck with cholera." The man wiped his forehead with a dirty handkerchief.

Adam had motioned for the hoagie to stop the mules at the lock. "Be best if you passed on through," the lock tender said.

"Can't do that," Adam said. "Have several passengers to pick up."

"No one is here to board."

"They'll be at the next lock in a half hour. That's the schedule." Adam swatted at several mosquitoes.

"Do as you will," the lock tender called. "Remember, I warned you."

And remember Adam did, as once through the stagnant water of the lock he and his crew, and his four passengers on board felt the sting of a foreboding silence. Muffled, but unmistakable, they heard the wailing of human voices.

"Do you think we ought to stop?" An alarmed crewmember mustered up the courage to ask. His voice quivered, but it wasn't the Captain that he was afraid of.

"Don't think we should, but I've promised a stop," Adam said, now uneasily aware of the cholera epidemic.

Adam looked at his crew and passengers. "What do you think?" he asked with a frightened feeling of his own.

Without willing them, the words "Don't stop," passed through the lips of one passenger. Adam felt nervous sweat run down from his armpits into his clothes.

"I think you're right. We'll go on," said Adam, swatting at another mosquito. He motioned to his mule driver. "Keep on movin'," he called, and *The New Ohio* continued on through the stagnant water.

❀ ❀ ❀

A stooped man, his back bent, a stick of wood supporting him said, "I was in Minster two days ago. They're burying them four tiers at a time in trenches seven feet wide. No funeral service, no nothin'." There was fear in his eyes.

Intense fear suddenly gripped Adam. The people were talking about the Minster cholera epidemic. Alese was there, in Minster, the same place that the people were talking about. The cholera was in other places, too, but she was there, helping a friend of the family, whose time for giving birth was close at hand.

His innards felt like jelly. What would he do if he lost Alese? Uncontrollably he shivered.

The meeting broke up. Still people stood around talking, feeling helpless.

"My sister wrote that some people are turning away from their neighbors and even their own family." a woman said, hugging herself, panic sounding in her voice.

"One family put their sick child in a room and watched it through a window. When it died, they left town. Can you imagine," the woman said, "not burying your own child!" Tears ran down her face.

Adam felt his own fear rise up as bile. *I've got to get to Alese,* he thought. *The New Ohio is not fast enough.* "I must take Sam." He muttered to himself as he pushed his way out of the meeting house into the bright morning sunlight. His knees felt wobbly as he mounted Sam.

To a member of his crew, who had come out behind him, he said, "Tell Mr. Charles how bad this cholera is, and tell him I'm on my way to get Alese. I'll follow the canal."

He rode hard the rest of the day. By evening he turned west to the edge of Minster. Behind him he heard the wailing of human voices. As he dismounted a man called out warningly. "We're struck with cholera. Better leave while you can."

He met Alese at the door. She looked tired, but well. She also looked frightened. Her fright caused the fear, which had subsided when he saw her at the door, to return.

He looked at her and then held her tightly. Her sobs were muffled in his clothing.

"It's terrible," she said blowing her nose. "There are so many sick."

"I'm taking you home," he said.

"I can't leave without Mary and Tom. Oh, and their precious new baby, Rebecca. Can they come?"

"I rode Sam. Do they have a wagon and a horse?" As he spoke Tom came to the door.

"Let's close the door," he said. "I have a wagon. With your help we can be ready to go in the morning," he said.

"What can I do?" Adam asked.

"How much can we take?" Alese asked.

"A mattress for Mary and the baby," said Tom. "We'll take blankets and necessary food. "Can we give you a bite to eat?" he asked Adam

"Don't take the time," he said.

"We must eat as well, so please join us. We'll plan as we eat."

Adam could see no fault in that thinking. As soon as the meal was finished he and Tom went to the barn out behind their house, and got the wagon cleaned out and ready for travel. They fed the one horse they owned, as well as Sam with grain, and well water. "Rest," he told them. "You'll have a heavy load to carry soon."

By early morning they were on their way. The horse pulled the wagon carrying Tom, Mary, and Rebecca, as well as necessary household items, Mary's rocking chair, and Tom's carpentry tools. Alese rode with Adam on Sam.

Staying away from villages, where the cholera was the most prevalent, made travel slower, but safer. That evening they found cover from the night inside a barn that they were given permission to use. The people who lived in the house brought out warm soup and fresh bread and left it at the barn door. Amicably they welcomed the tired travelers, and encouraged them to use their fresh well water, but the neighborliness was all from a distance.

Fear that they might carry the disease kept each away from the other. The owners of the barn stood on their porch and talked loudly, conversing. They told how they had taken in their niece and nephew to raise as their own. The one- and two-year-old children's parents had died of cholera two weeks earlier.

Tom and Mary were unable to continue hiding their fear, and openly held each other as they cried. Adam and Alese were grateful to be going back home. They arrived the next afternoon, tired and dirty, but happy to be there.

Margaret, Andrew, Mr. Charles, and Mrs. Elizabeth all came hurrying out of the back door of the house to welcome them. Adam was overwhelmed with the love he felt for these people who he'd known for the past eleven years. He knew he would feel a terrible loss without them.

"I'm so happy you came here to us, Margaret said to Tom and Mary. She oohed and aahed over the baby.

Seeing the carpenter tools in the wagon Mr. Charles said, "Margaret has told us so much about you, though she never said you were a carpenter. That is your trade?"

"Yes, sir. I'm a carpenter. If we can stay until I can find work, we'd be grateful."

"I've needed a carpenter for some time, and I know of other work you can find."

"Can they stay in the two spare rooms across the hall from Andrew?" Margaret asked. "Until they can go back home when the cholera is gone?"

"I don't see why not," Mr. Charles said. "Now let's get you folks in the house. Margaret, could you get them something to eat?" Adam and Alese had dismounted and stood beside the wagon to help.

"Andrew and Adam, let's go upstairs and move a few things around to make those rooms livable. Alese, please, bring up the linens."

CHAPTER 8
1849
Blended Families

Later, after everyone had eaten, and the guests were settled in their two rooms on the second floor, Adam and Mr. Charles sat in the library.

"I know I've slacked off on my boat duties," Adam said.

"You did, but with good reason," Mr. Charles said. "I would have done the same. Almost no boats are running. *The New Ohio* should not be either. The cholera risk to you and your crew is far too great."

"I think so, too," said Adam. He got up from his chair and walked to the open window covered with thin cloth to keep out the mosquitoes. Pulling back the cloth he looked out at the sunset. "That is the only thing of beauty this evening," he pointed to the golden orange hues.

"We've had bad times before. We'll get through this, God willing." Mr. Charles said. He looked at Adam and asked, "What is bothering you, Adam?"

"I haven't been home to see my family," he stopped for a moment. "It's strange to refer to my Aunt and Uncle's family as my family and their home as my home. Right now I feel as though your family, and Alese's are my family and this is home.

He swallowed hard. "What I want to do is to go to see them. See if they're well, and let them know that we are. Ask if they need any help and if they do, I'd like to do for them what I can."

"They must be worried about you," Mr. Charles said. "I think you should go see them. You have a blended family. Some people never have a place to call home, nor anyone to call family, yet you have two of each. How fortunate you are."

Adam nodded, realizing then, that he once had been one of those people, who had had no home, and no family.

"I haven't talked to Alese yet about my going, but I'd like to leave in the morning."

"Take Andrew with you. I'll talk to Margaret. She and Alese will be busy with baby Rebecca and Mary. Alese can stay here while you're away if she'd like.

"Tom can help me while you are gone." He walked to the window and put his arm around Adam's shoulder. "Stay as long as you need, but come home as soon as you can. We will all be worried about both of you."

Adam and Alese rode to their own home at the end of Mr. Charles' lane. After bedding down Sam in their small barn, Adam walked to the house.

"It's so good to be home," Alese told him as she put her arms around him. "I had such fear in Minster until I saw you at the doorway."

He put his arms around her, holding her. "I don't know what I'd do without you," he said, kissing her.

She looked up into his eyes, tears sparkling in her own. "I don't know what I would do without you," she said lifting her hand and lightly touching the scar on his chin. Her fingers moved to his lips.

He took her fingers in his hand and kissed them tenderly. "I love you," he said and kissed her lips.

Later he told her of his plan to leave early in the morning, to see his uncle and aunt.

"We've only just gotten back," she said, disappointment sounding in her voice.

"I feel I must go," he said. "They need to know that we, and your family are well, and I need to know that they are."

"You do need to go," she said after a time. "I don't want them to worry like we did. In Minster they were burying people in the same graves, not just one, but up to six people, some covered only with a shroud. They ran out of coffins. What if they think you might have Cholera?" She said. "You must go. They need to know you're safe."

In the morning, she waved goodbye to Andrew and Adam as they left, determined not to worry, but wanting them home before they had even left.

CHAPTER 9
Spring 1850
"Bet Me"

The still water rippled as *The New Ohio* glided north under mule power. They were less than one hundred miles from Toledo, as the milestone marker, stuck on the west side of the Canal and standing up on the towpath, attested.

Ten Mile Woods, soon to be known as Delphos, sat on the bank of the canal, and had two hotels and a boarding house. Two of Adam's passengers would spend some time at the boarding house. They had relatives they were to meet, and would catch another boat going back south in a week or two.

Adam watched as his two passengers were greeted by a man in clerical garb standing at the bank.

"Father Bredeick," the man said introducing himself to the passengers. His dark hair worn below his ears also touched his collar in the back. He held out his hand to them. He was of medium stature, with wide-set dark eyes.

The priest directed the two passengers to the boarding house.

Adam called for Andrew to come with him, to give themselves as well as the other passengers, a break. When they got off the boat, the Roman Catholic priest was still there to greet them.

"My name's Adam Miller. This is Andrew Reed. "Andrew held out his hand.

"Welcome to our settlement. You've been here before?"

"I have," Adam said. "This is the first time for Andrew."

"What do you think of the settlement?" he asked Adam.

"It's certainly a growing place. I understand you're putting in corduroy roads. Someone said you have a newspaper as well?"

The priest nodded his head. "The newspaper's called *The Section Ten Budget*. Judge Metcalfe is the publisher. We're quite proud of him, and of the paper."

"I would think so," Adam said as he looked around. "Though, I've not seen any of your corduroy roads."

"They're not laid yet, but hopefully by next year. Our settlement roads aren't the best either; most are low and full of stumps. Occasionally we throw slabs of stone in mud holes or throw planks across them. We have so much to do here."

The priest stood quietly for a moment looking at the canal, then at them. "Is there something I can help you with?"

"We're hoping to find some place to get a good, hot, cooked meal."

"We can help you with that," the priest said with a smile. "At the hotel," he said pointing to the building along the street.

"Thank you," Adam and Andrew said in unison, smiles appearing on their faces. As they walked, they saw the beginning growth of a town. At a further distance they saw trees being felled one at a time.

The entry door of the long, two-storied hotel opened into the middle of the dining room. Six sets of wooden tables, each of them with three or four chairs, invited people to sit. Adam and Andrew did so. A hot noonday meal of sausage, bread, and fried potatoes was just what they wanted.

At the table next to them a stern-faced woman sat across from her husband. Her light-red hair, parted in the middle and pulled into a bun at the back of her head made her face look tight. Her hands were red. *So many women have hands that are cracked and even bleeding,* Adam thought and wondered, *Will Alese's hands look like theirs in a few years?*

Three men came in, wearing dark pants and unbuttoned jackets. As they sat down at another table beside them, each draped his jacket on the back of his chair.

"I never saw anything like it," said the shortest of the men. "There could be a lot of land cleared using that slashing method."

The heavy-set man of the trio said, "I watched the wood chopper the day before yesterday. He chopped into those trees, all on the same side, and just enough so that they'd no longer be sturdy. Along came the wind yesterday, and they fell like…well I don't know what, but once the first ones fell where the wind hit them, they just knocked down all the others that had been slashed."

"We'll have no trouble selling cleared land," said the short man.

"You mean Father Bredeick will have no trouble selling his land," the tall thin man said appreciatively.

"No matter how much he sells, he'll just give some of the money back to the settlement," said the heavy man whose shirt button had just popped open. "Did you know his brother Ferdinand gave some of his money back, too?"

"Both do it to help cover the cost of the canal construction, and to help this town grow," added the shorter man.

"At two-dollars-and-fifty cents an acre for land five miles on either side of the canal, and a dollar-and-twenty-five cents an acre for any other land, the cost of construction of the canal will soon be paid for," the tall man said.

"And the soil is so rich. It's better than in Verl, Germany," said the short man. "As soon as we get the drainage problems solved we'll be just fine."

"We have different problems here, compared to those we had back in Germany," said the heavier man. "Here, even with land clearing, drainage problems, and so much building to be done, besides adjusting to the weather, we are fortunate as we have our own land, and are free from that absolute political domination!"

Adam reached into his pocket for the money to pay for his meal.

An hour later, Adam and Andrew were again on the job, and had already gone through the Delphos Lock 23, an easily manageable lock made of wood, with a drop of seven and one-half feet. As they approached Lock 24, made of stone, they had to wait for the boat already in the lock to exit before they could enter.

Further up the canal they crossed the wooden Jennings Creek Aqueduct. Shortly afterwards they made their way up to the Ottoville Lock 28.

Twenty-one miles to the north *The New Ohio* docked before reaching Junction. It had gone past Flatrock Creek Aqueduct, where the Wabash and Erie Canals joined. At this point, Adam took on supplies, and crates were exchanged. As they worked, clouds moved in, and a southern wind began to blow.

Captain Adam had several times run into trouble at Junction, so before arriving there, along with the supplies he'd taken on, he hired an extra hand called a roughneck. The man wore his beard scraggly. He was rough-looking, and his manner seemed threatening. For a short time he stood quietly near Adam and Andrew holding one of the eight foot poles used on the boat. After a spell he strutted about the deck.

He stopped and stood beside the two women passengers that had gotten on at Ten Mile Woods. They were on their way to Lake Erie. Upon his approach the women moved closer together and looked toward where Adam stood.

"I wouldn't hurt a hair on either of your heads," he said trying to put them at ease. "Only gonna be here a bit." He shaped his hardened hands into fists. "Gonna knock a few hard heads together, and kick a few butts into the canal, just to cool them off, of course. Then I'll be off."

It was late afternoon as *The New Ohio* passed two other canal boats. Time was vital as Adam had to be in the lead, and get through the lock first, to get past Junction and Lock 33, north of Defiance before nightfall.

Another freighter came up behind *The New Ohio* trying to pass them and butt in, as Adam was setting up to go through the lock.

Adam's roughneck stood at the foredeck spoiling for a fight. "We can't wait any longer, Capt'n," the roughneck yelled. "We gotta go through first or we'll be stuck here til daybreak."

"We're going through now," Adam said forcefully. He'd been bullied before.

The roughneck took charge yelling at the two men on the freighter. "Get your mule-eared faces out of that tub, and up on the bank. I'll take on both of you. The winner goes through first." He hopped from *The New Ohio* and scampered up to the top of the bank and stood, his legs spread, feet firmly planted. "I'm waiting!" he said.

That was all he had time to say before the two men from the freight boat jumped on the bank and rushed him. The force of them almost caused the roughneck to lose his footing.

It was then that the first bolt of lightning electrified the air. A crack of thunder muffled the sounds of the fight. When the rain drops began to fall the fight was over. With a grin the roughneck jumped into the boat saying, "Let's go, Capt'n, afore they close the lock."

Adam had already motioned to his hoagie to move the mules up the towpath in order to pull *The New Ohio* close to the towpath, preparing it to enter the lock.

The other freight boat, no longer trying to pass them, stayed on the opposite side of the canal. Its team of mules moved to the far side of the towpath as their hoagie gave slack to the freight's towline, letting it sink into the water. *The New Ohio* passed over the sinking towline, on the right side of the freight boat, and pulled into the lock.

The men who had been knocked into the canal stood along the freight boat railing with water dripping off them, angrily muttering, and glaring at the roughneck. One of them yelled. "We'll get you the next time."

The roughneck, taking a tough stance at the front of the boat smugly hollered back, "Bet me!"

THE END

EPILOGUE

Time continued on in the wilderness passageway. The life of Adam and Alese changed as they became the parents of two sons.

Andrew, who had always helped Mr. Charles, became the overseer of his farm. Alese continued to keep Mr. Charles' records.

Samuel Waite eventually married Margaret, Alese and Andrew's mother. Adam sold his land in the Black Swamp in 1846 after the canal was through.

There are many items of interest that were not in this story. Some as follows:

In 1845 the canal opened for through traffic from the Ohio River to Lake Erie. It covered a distance of around 265 miles. At its highest point (the summit), the canal was approximately 512 feet above the Ohio River. Lock 1 at New Bremen is on a water plateau called the North American Continental Divide.

Before the canal was dug the planned mileage for feeders was around 25 miles. One of those feeders was the Sidney feeder, which covered fourteen miles and brought water to the main canal from the Great Miami River.

Part of the difficulty of getting the canal dug through from the Ohio River to Lake Erie was the cutting through of a stone shelf in an area named Deep Cut. It is located between Kossuth and Spencerville, an area 6,600 feet long and 52 feet deep.

The canal helped farmers by getting better prices for their goods, enabling them to pay less for their purchased goods, helping them to drain some of their land, and bringing in more settlers.

Glossary

Aqueduct A watertight wooden trough, used to carry canal boats over a large body of water (like a river.) These had to be built sturdy and watertight since they had to carry the same amount of water as the canal channel did. Some aqueducts had roofs which made them look like a covered bridge. There were 19 aqueducts along the Miami-Erie Canal.

Berlin renamed Ft. Loramie

Black Swamp Area Starts at the northwest corner of Ohio and goes over to Lake Erie; then a straight line south, from between Toledo and Port Clinton down to Auglaize County from Lake St. Marys to Indiana.

Boats were the property of either individuals or of companies organized for the purpose of operating them.

Canal lock constructed of stone or of timber. Was 90 feet long and 15 feet wide with walls five feet thick at the bottom, and four feet at the waterline. There were 103 locks along the Miami-Erie Canal.

Canal name The canal underwent a name change during its existence. When first built the section between Cincinnati to Dayton was called the Miami Canal. The section from Dayton north to Maumee was called the Miami Extension Canal. Later when it reached Lake Erie it was called the Miami-Erie Canal.

Canal sections At the Cincinnati end the Miami Canal was authorized in Feb. 1825, and went from 32 miles north of St. Marys, including a 12 mile "deep cut" above St. Marys. The Miami Extension Canal was authorized in Feb. of 1831.

At the Lake Erie end the Wabash and Erie Canal was authorized Feb. 1833.

Cargo boat A type of freight boat.

Commission Merchants They assembled cargos for shipment. After adding transportation costs, the brokers sold the products at higher prices in bigger cities such as Cincinnati.

Continental North American Divide The town of New Breman is located here, on the Loramie Summit. It is the southern-most town where the water flows north.

Corduroy roads made of logs laid side by side on the road and attached to each other by wooden stringers. This was used to give soggy, muddy roads solidity.

Crew (boat) Two or three assistants to the captain, two of those being the steersman. There were also young boys who were the mule drivers. These boys were called hoagies. They took care of the animals and drove the mules on the towpath.

Culvert A type of cement bridge used by the canal to cross over a small body of water.

Delphos A settlement originally called Ten Mile Woods. It sat on the banks of the canal north of St. Marys.

Dry docks Privately owned businesses for the purpose of building, repairing and storing canal boats.

Father Bredeick Reverand John Otto Bredeick was born January 23, 1794 in Verl, Germany. He was ordained as a priest in 1822. He came to Ohio to Ten Mile Woods (Delphos) in 1844. In 1848 he founded Ottoville.

Feeder canals (channels) A short canal which branched off the main canal. Constructed to bring water into the canal and sometimes dug to supply transportation service to a particular area.

Freight boat Transported lumber, stone, grain, and other items that were non-perishable.

Hoagie Young boy who drove the mules on the towpath.

Guard lock Built at the mouth of a dock or basin to hold water, in order to prevent flooding.

Inland Water system Another name for the canal system.

Line Boat Carried both passengers and freight.

Mule Skinner A name for an adult hoagie.

Night travel Many boats traveled at night but were required to carry a lantern, both at the front and the rear of their boat.

Packet boat A combination passenger, diner, sleeper, and mail boat.

Reservoirs Artificial lakes. There were three close to the summit area. They were Grand Lake St. Marys, Indian Lake, and Lake Loramie.

St. Marys feeder Ran from Grand Lake St. Marys to the canal. It transported water to the canal.

Sidecut Intended to provide direct access from the canal to a certain area.

Slackwater navigation Poling or towing a boat across an area where the level of the canal was not that much different from an intersecting waterway.

Sluice gate or Wicket gate A gate below water level on the lock gate. It either let water into the lock or out of the lock.

Towpath Path ten feet wide that ran on one side of the canal. The berm (also known as the heel) was on the other side, and was five feet wide.

Turnaround A large area of water in which canal boats could turn around or be repaired.

❀ ❀ ❀

This story was first started in my mind when, as a child, I walked in a wide, four-foot to five-foot area that bordered the edge of my grandfather's land. The canal had been filled in, so it was no longer four feet deep, but was perhaps a foot lower than the rest of the land. It occasionally still held rain water and grew a cattail or two.

Along the property where I went to school, there was, what I believed to be, a canal feeder. The water was only a small stream. Buttercups, grass, and weeds grew on the slope of the bank. I'd been known to pick some of those butter cups, and since I thought this to be part of a canal feeder I wondered what the Miami and Erie Canal was all about.

Years later, after having moved many times, mostly in areas where the Miami and Erie Canal had existed, I started to read whatever books I could find about the canal. My mother's old newspaper clippings, many articles, and many more books, (mostly out of print and found only in the libraries), helped me to decide that I must write this book.

It has been an enormous undertaking, as I had no idea how many pages I would have to read and study before I could write about the canal knowledgeably.

My main reason for writing this book was to help us remember how important this one long passageway, through the wilderness of Ohio, was to the growth of our country.

Suggested Reading List

A Historical and Descriptive Study of the Miami and Erie Canal. By Eichenauer.

A History of Northwest Ohio By Nevin O. Winter, Litt. D. The Lewis Publishing Co, Chicago and New York. 1917.

A Photo Album of Ohio's Canal Era 1825-1913 by Jack Giecke. The Kent State University Press.

Miami and Erie: Canal, Commerce and History. Copyright 1990 by The Delphos Canal Commission.

Ohio Canals by Frank Trevorrow.

Old Towpaths by Alvin F. Harlow. Kennikat Press Inc. Port Washington, New York.

Tales from Great-Grandpa's Trunk by Glenna Meckstroth. Copyright 1998.

The Foot of the Rapids by Marilyn Van Vooris Wendler. Maumee, Ohio 1838-1983.

The Ohio Canals by Frank Wilcox. Kent State University Press-1969

The Ohio Story by Frank Siedel. Copyright 1950. Published by the World Publishing Co.

Printed in the United States
84190LV00002B/78/A